A Pakeha Maori

Old New Zealand

A Tale of the Good Old Times

A Pakeha Maori

Old New Zealand
A Tale of the Good Old Times

ISBN/EAN: 9783337073343

Printed in Europe, USA, Canada, Australia, Japan

Cover: Foto ©Andreas Hilbeck / pixelio.de

More available books at **www.hansebooks.com**

OLD NEW ZEALAND;

A Tale of the Good Old Times.

BY

A PAKEHA MAORI.

"Of Anthropophagi, and men whose heads
Do grow BETWEEN their shoulders."

Second Edition.

AUCKLAND :

ROBERT J. CREIGHTON & ALFRED SCALES, QUEEN STREET.

PREFACE.

To the English reader, and to most of those who have arrived in New Zealand within the last thirty years, it may be necessary to state that the descriptions of Maori life and manners of past times found in these sketches owe nothing to fiction. The different scenes and incidents are given exactly as they occurred, and all the persons described are real persons.

Contact with the British settlers has of late years effected a marked and rapid change in the manners and mode of life of the natives, and the Maori of the present day are as unlike what they were when I first saw them as they are still unlike a civilised people or British subjects.

The writer has therefore thought it might be worth while to place a few sketches of old Maori life on record before the remembrance of them has quite passed away; though in doing so he has by no means exhausted an interesting subject, and a more full and particular delineation of old Maori life, manners, and history has yet to be written.

CONTENTS.

CHAPTER I.

CHAPTER II.

CHAPTER III.

CHAPTER VIII.

CHAPTER IX.

CHAPTER X.

CHAPTER XI.

CHAPTER XII.

CHAPTER XIII.

CHAPTER XIV.

CHAPTER XV.

OLD NEW ZEALAND.

CHAPTER I.

INTRODUCTORY—FIRST VIEW OF NEW ZEALAND—FIRST SIGHT
OF THE NATIVES, AND FIRST SENSATIONS EXPERIENCED
BY A MERE PAKEHA—A MAORI CHIEF'S NOTIONS OF
TRADING IN THE OLD TIMES—A DISSERTATION ON
'COURAGE'—A FEW WORDS ON DRESS—THE CHIEF'S
SOLILOQUY—THE MAORI CRY OF WELCOME.

AH! those good old times, when first I
came to New Zealand, we shall never see
their like again. Since then the world seems
to have gone wrong somehow. A dull sort
of world this now. The very sun does not
seem to me to shine as bright as it used.
Pigs and potatoes have degenerated; and
everything seems "flat, stale, and unprofit-
able." But those were the times!—the
"good old times"—before Governors were
invented, and law, and justice, and all that.

B

When every one did as he liked,—except
when his neighbours would not let him, (the
more shame for them,)—when there were no
taxes, or duties, or public works, or public
to require them. Who cared then whether
he owned a coat?—or believed in shoes or
stockings? The men were bigger and stouter
in those days; and the women,—ah! Money
was useless and might go a begging. A
sovereign was of no use except to make a
hole in and hang it in a child's ear. The
few I brought went that way, and I have
seen them swapped for shillings, which
were thought more becoming. What cared
I? A fish-hook was worth a dozen of them,
and I had lots of fish-hooks. Little did I
think in those days that I should ever see
here towns and villages, banks and insurance
offices, prime ministers and bishops; and hear
sermons preached, and see men hung, and all
the other plagues of civilization. I am a
melancholy man. I feel somehow as if I had
got older. I am no use in these dull times.
I mope about in solitary places, exclaiming
often, "Oh! where are those good old times?"
and echo, or some young Maori whelp from
the Three Kings, answers from behind a
bush,—No HEA.

I shall not state the year in which I first saw the mountains of New Zealand appear above the sea ; there is a false suspicion getting about that I am growing old. This must be looked down, so I will at present avoid dates. I always held a theory that time was of no account in New Zealand, and I do believe I was right up to the time of the arrival of the first Governor. The natives hold this opinion still, especially those who are in debt : so I will just say it was in the good old times, long ago, that, from the deck of a small trading schooner in which I had taken my passage from somewhere, I first cast eyes on Maori land. It *was* Maori land then ; but alas ! what is it now ? Success to you, O King of Waikato. May your *mana* never be less !—long may you hold at bay the demon of civilization, though fall at last *I fear you must. Plutus with golden hoof is trampling on your landmarks. He mocks the war-song ; but should *I* see your fall, at least one Pakeha Maori shall raise the *tangi* ; and with flint and shell as of old shall the women lament you.

Let me, however, leave these melancholy thoughts for a time, forget the present, take courage, and talk about the past. I have not

got on shore yet ; a thing I must accomplish
as a necessary preliminary to looking about
me, and telling what I saw.   I do not understand the pakeha way of beginning a story in
the middle ; so to start fair, I must fairly get
on shore, which, I am surprised to find, was
easier to *do* than to describe.

The little schooner neared the land, and as
we came closer and closer, I began in a most
unaccountable manner to remember all the
tales I had ever heard of people being baked
in ovens, with cabbage and potato "fixins."
I had before this had some considerable experience of "savages," but as they had no regular system of domestic cookery of the nature
I have hinted at, and being, as I was in those
days, a mere pakeha (a character I have since
learned to despise), I felt, to say the least,
rather curious as to the then existing demand
on shore for butchers' meat.

The ship sailed on, and I went below
and loaded my pistols ; not that I expected
at all to conquer the country with them,
but somehow because I could not help it.
We soon came to anchor in a fine harbour
before the house of the very first settler
who had ever entered it, and to this time
he was the only one.   He had, however, a

few Europeans in his employ; and there was at some forty miles distance a sort of nest of English, Irish, Scotch, Dutch, French, and American, runaways from South Sea whalers, with whom were also congregated certain other individuals of the pakeha race, whose manner of arrival in the country was not clearly accounted for, and to enquire into which was, as I found afterwards, considered extremely impolite, and a great breach of *bienséance*. They lived in a half savage state, or to speak correctly, in a savage and-a-half state, being greater savages by far than the natives themselves.

I must, however, turn back a little, for I perceive I am not on shore yet.

The anchoring of a vessel of any size, large or small, in a port of New Zealand, in those days, was an event of no small importance ; and, accordingly, from the deck we could see the shore crowded by several hundreds of natives, all in a great state of excitement, shouting and running about, many with spears and clubs in their hands, and altogether looking to the inexperienced new-comer very much as if they were speculating on an immediate change of diet. I must say these at least were my impressions on seeing the

mass of shouting, gesticulating, tattooed fellows, who were exhibiting before us, and who
all seemed to be mad with excitement of
some sort or other. Shortly after we came
to anchor, a boat came off, in which was
Mr. —, the settler I have mentioned, and
also the principal chief of the tribe of
natives inhabiting this part of the country.
Mr. — gave me a hearty welcome to New
Zealand, and also an invitation to his house,
telling me I was welcome to make it my home
for any unlimited time, till I had one of
my own. The chief also,—having made some
enquiries first of the captain of the schooner,
such as whether I was a *rangatira*, if I
had plenty of *taonga* (goods) on board, and
other particulars ; and having been answered
by the Captain in the most satisfactory
manner,—came up to me and gave me a most
sincere welcome. (I love sincerity). He
would have welcomed me, however, had I
been as poor as Job, for pakehas were, in
those days, at an enormous premium. Even
Job, at the worst, (a *pakeha* Job) might be
supposed to have an old coat, or a spike
nail, or a couple of iron hoops left on hand,
and these were "good trade" in the times
I speak of ; and under a process well under-

stood at the time by my friend the chief, were sure to change hands soon after his becoming aware of their whereabouts. His idea of trade was this :—He took them, and never paid for them till he took something else of greater value, which, whatever it might be, he never paid for till he made a third still heavier haul. He always paid just what he thought fit to give, and when he chose to withdraw his patronage from any pakeha who might be getting too knowing for him, and extend it to some newer arrival, he never paid for the last "lot of trade;" but, to give him his due, he allowed his pakeha friends to make the best bargain they could with the rest of the tribe, with the exception of a few of his nearest relations, over whose interests he would watch. So, after all, the pakeha would make a living; but I have never heard of one of the old traders who got rich by trading with the natives : there were too many drawbacks of the nature I have mentioned, as well as others unnecessary to mention just yet, which prevented it.

I positively vow and protest to you, gentle and patient reader, that if ever I get safe on shore, I will do my best to give you satisfaction ; let me get once on shore, and I am all right : but unless I get my feet on *terra firma*, how can I ever begin my tale of the good old times ? As long as I am on board ship I am cramped and crippled, and a mere slave to Greenwich time, and can't get on. Some people, I am aware, would make a dash at it, and manage the thing without the aid of boat, canoe, or life preserver ; but such people are, for the most part, dealers in fiction, which I am not : my story is a true story, not " founded on fact," but fact itself, and so I cannot manage to get on shore a moment sooner than circumstances will permit. It may be that I ought to have landed before this; but I must confess I don't know any more about the right way to tell a story, than a native minister knows how to " come " a war dance. I declare the mention of the war dance calls up a host of reminiscences, pleasurable and painful, exhilarating and depressing, in such a way as no one but a few, a very few, pakeha Maori, can understand. Thunder !—but no ; let me get ashore ; how can I dance on the water, or before I ever knew how ? On shore I will get this time, I am determined, in spite of fate—so now for it.

The boat of my friend Mr. — being about to return to the shore, leaving the chief and Mr. — on board, and I seeing the thing had to be done, plucked up courage, and having secretly felt the priming of my pistols under my coat, got into the boat.

I must here correct myself. I have said "plucked up courage," but that is not exactly my meaning The fact is, kind reader, if you have followed me thus far, you are about to be rewarded for your perseverance. I am determined to make you as wise as I am my-self on at least one important subject, and that is not saying a little, let me inform you, as I can hardly suppose you have made the discovery for yourself on so short an ac-quaintance. Falstaff, who was a very clever fellow, and whose word cannot be doubted, says—"The better part of valour is discretion." Now, that being the case, what in the name of Achilles, Hector, and Colonel Gold (*he*, I mean *Achilles*, was a rank coward, who went about knocking people on the head, being himself next thing to invulnerable, and who could not be hurt till he turned his back to the enemy. There is a deep moral in this same story about Achilles which perhaps, by and bye, I may explain to you)—what, I say again, in the name of everything valorous, can the worser part of valour be, if "discretion" be the better? The fact is, my dear sir, I don't believe in courage at all, nor ever did; but there is something far better, which has carried me through many serious scrapes with *éclât* and safety; I mean the appearance of courage. If you have this you may drive the world before you. As for real courage, I do not believe there can be any such thing. A man who sees himself in danger of being killed by his enemy and is not in a precious fright, is simply not courageous but mad. The man who is not frightened because he cannot see the danger, is a person of weak mind—a fool—who ought to be locked up lest he walk into a well with eyes open; but the appearance of courage, or rather, as I deny the existence of the thing itself, that appearance which is thought to be courage, that is the thing will carry you through!—get you made K.C.B., Victoria Cross, and all that! Men by help of this quality do the most heroic actions, being all the time ready to die of mere fright, but keeping up a good countenance all the time. Here is the secret —pay attention, it is worth much money— if ever you get into any desperate battle or skirmish, and feel in such a state of mortal fear that you almost wish to be shot to get rid of it, just say to yourself--"If I am so preciously frightened, what must the other fellow be?" The thought will refresh you; your own self-esteem will answer that of course the enemy is more frightened than you are, consequently, the nearer you feel to running away the more reason you have to stand. Look at the last gazette of the last victory, where thousands of men at one shilling *per diem*, minus certain very serious deductions, "covered themselves with glory." The thing is clear : the other fellows ran first, and that is all about it ! My secret is a very good secret ; but one must of course do the thing properly ; no matter of what kind the danger is, you must look it boldly in the face and keep your wits about you, and the more frightened you get the more determined you must be--to keep up appearances—and half the danger is gone at once. So now, having corrected myself, as well as given some valuable advice, I shall start again for the shore by saying that I plucked up a very good appearance of courage and got on board the boat.

For the honor and glory of the British

nation, of which I considered myself in some
degree a representative on this momentous
occasion, I had dressed myself in one of my
best suits.   My frock coat was, I fancy, "the
thing ;" my waistcoat was the result of much
and deep thought, in cut, colour, and material—I may venture to affirm that the like
had not been often seen in the southern
hemisphere.   My tailor has, as I hear, long
since realised a fortune and retired, in consequence of the enlightenment he at different
times received from me on the great principles of, not clothing, but embellishing the
human subject.   My hat looked down criticism, and my whole turn out such as I
calculated would " astonish the natives," and
cause awe and respect for myself individually
and the British nation in general, of whom I
thought fit to consider myself no bad sample.
Here I will take occasion to remark that
some attention to ornament and elegance in
the matter of dress is not only allowable but
commendable.   Man is the only beast to
whom a discretionary power has been left in
this respect : why then should he not take a
hint from nature, and endeavour to beautify
his person ? Peacocks and birds of paradise
could no doubt live and get fat though all

their feathers were the colour of a Quaker's
leggings, but see how they are ornamented!
Nature has, one would say, exhausted herself
in beautifying them. Look at the tiger and
leopard! Could not they murder without
their stripes and spots?—but see how their
coats are painted! Look at the flowers—at
the whole universe—and you will see every-
where the ornamental combined with the
useful. Look, then, to the cut and colour
of your coat, and do not laugh at the Maori
of past times, who, not being "seized" of a
coat because he has never been able to seize
one, carves and tattoos legs, arms, and face.

The boat is, however, darting towards the
shore, rapidly propelled by four stout natives.
My friend —— and the chief are on board.
The chief has got his eye on my double gun,
which is hanging up in the cabin. He takes
it down and examines it closely. He is a good
judge of a gun. It is the best *tupara* he has
ever seen, and his speculations run something
very like this:—"A good gun, a first-rate
gun; I must have this; I must *tapu* it before
I leave the ship; [here he pulls a piece of
the fringe from his cloak and ties it round the
stock of the gun, thereby rendering it impossible for me to sell, give away, or dispose of it

in any way to anyone but himself] I wonder
what the pakeha will want for it! I will
promise him as much flax or as many pigs as
ever he likes for it. True, I have no flax just
now, and am short of pigs, they were almost
all killed at the last *hahunga*; but if he is in
a hurry he can buy the flax or pigs from the
people, which ought to satisfy him. Perhaps
he would take a piece of land !—that would be
famous. I would give him a piece quite close
to the *kainga*, where I would always have him
close to me ; I hope he may take the land ; then
I should have two pakehas, him and ——. All
the inland chiefs would envy me. This ——
is getting too knowing; he has taken to hiding
his best goods of late, and selling them before
I knew he had them. It's just the same as
thieving, and I won't stand it. He sold three
muskets the other day to the Ngatiwaki, and
I did not know he had them, or I should have
taken them. I could have paid for them some
time or another. It was wrong, wrong, very
wrong, to let that tribe have those muskets.
He is not their pakeha ; let them look for a
pakeha for themselves. Those Ngatiwaki are
getting too many muskets—those three make
sixty-four they have got besides two *tupara*.
Certainly we have a great many more, and

the Ngatiwaki are our relations, but then there was Kohu, we killed, and Patu, we stole his wife. There is no saying what these Ngatiwaki may do if they should get plenty of muskets ; they are game enough for anything. It was wrong to give them those muskets ; wrong, wrong, wrong !" After-experience enabled me to tell just what the chief's soliloquy was, as above.

But all this time the boat is darting to the shore, and as the distance is only a couple of hundred yards, I can hardly understand how it is that I have not yet landed. The crew are pulling like mad, being impatient to show the tribe the prize they have made,—a regular *pakeha rangatira* as well as a *rangatira pakeha*, (two very different things,) who has lots of tomahawks, and fish-hooks, and blankets, and a *tupara*, and is even suspected to be the owner of a great many "pots" of gunpowder ! " He is going to stop with the tribe, he is going to trade, he is going to be a pakeha *for us*." These last conclusions were, however, jumped at, the "pakeha" not having then any notions of trade or commerce, and being only inclined to look about and amuse himself. The boat nears the shore, and now arises from a hundred voices the call of welcome,—"*Haere mai! haere mai! hoe mai! hoe mai! haere mai, e-te-pa-ke-ha, haere mai!* mats, hands, and certain ragged petticoats put into requisition for that occasion, all at the same time waving in the air in sign of welcome. Then a pause. Then, as the boat came nearer, another burst of *haere mai!* But unaccustomed as I was then to the Maori salute, I disliked the sound. There was a wailing melancholy cadence that did not strike me as being the appropriate tone of welcome ; and, as I was quite ignorant up to this time of my own importance, wealth, and general value as a pakeha, I began, as the boat closed in with the shore, to ask myself whether possibly this same "*haere mai*" might not be the Maori for "dilly, dilly, come and be killed." There was, however, no help for it now ; we were close to the shore, and so, putting on the most unconcerned countenance possible, I prepared to make my *entrée* into Maori land in a proper and dignified manner.

CHAPTER II.

THE MARKET PRICE OF A PAKEHA—THE VALUE OF A
PAKEHA "AS SUCH"—MAORI HOSPITALITY IN THE
GOOD OLD TIMES—A RESPECTABLE FRIEND—MAORI
MERMAIDS—MY NOTIONS OF THE VALUE OF GOLD—
HOW I GOT ON SHORE.

HERE I must remark that in those days the
value of a pakeha to a tribe was enormous.
For want of pakehas to trade with, and from
whom to procure gunpowder and muskets,
many tribes or sections of tribes were about
this time exterminated or nearly so by their
more fortunate neighbours who got pakehas
before them, and who consequently became
armed with muskets first. A pakeha trader
was therefore of a value say about twenty
times his own weight in muskets. This,
according to my notes made at the time, I
find to have represented a value in New
Zealand something about what we mean in
England when we talk of the sum total of the
national debt. A book-keeper, or a second-
rate pakeha, not a trader, might be valued

at say his weight in tomakawks ; an
enormous sum also. The poorest labouring
pakeha, though he might have no property,
would earn something—his value to the chief
and tribe with whom he lived might be estimated at say his weight in fish-hooks, or
about a hundred thousand pounds or so;
value estimated by eagerness to obtain the
article.

The value of a musket was not to be estimated to a native by just what he gave for
it : he gave all he had, or could procure, and
had he ten times as much to give he would
have given it, if necessary, or if not, he would
buy ten muskets instead of one. Muskets !
muskets ! muskets ! nothing but muskets, was
the first demand of the Maori ; muskets and
gunpowder at any cost.

I do not, however, mean to affirm 'that
pakehas were at this time valued "as such,"
—like Mr. Pickwick's silk stockings, which
were very good and valuable stockings, "as
stockings"—not at all. A loose straggling
pakeha—a runaway from a ship for instance,—
who had nothing, and was never likely to have
anything, a vagrant straggler passing from
place to place,—was not of much account even
in those times. Two men of this description

(runaway sailors) were hospitably entertained one night by a chief, a very particular friend of mine, who, to pay himself for his trouble and outlay, eat one of them next morning. Remember, my good reader, I don't deal in fiction ; my friend eat the pakeha sure enough, and killed him before he eat him, which was civil, for it was not always done But then, certainly, the pakeha was a *tutua*, a nobody, a fellow not worth a spike nail ; no one knew him ; he had no relations, no goods, no expectations, no anything : what could be made of him ? Of what use on earth was he except to eat ? And, indeed, not much good even for that—they say he was not good meat. But good well-to-do pakehas, traders, ship captains, labourers, or employers of labour, these were to be honoured, cherished, caressed, protected, and plucked. Plucked judiciously, (the Maori is a clever fellow in his way,) so that the feathers might grow again. But as for poor, mean, mere, *Pakeha tutua,—e aha te pai?*

Before going any farther I beg to state that I hope the English reader or the new-comer, who does not understand Maori morality—especially of the glorious old time—will not form a bad opinion of my

friend's character, merely because he eat a
good-for-nothing sort of pakeha, who really
was good for nothing else. People from
the old countries I have often observed to
have a kind of over-delicacy about them,
the result of a too effeminate course of life
and over-civilization, which is the cause
that, often starting from premises which
are true enough, they will, being carried
away by their over-sensitive constitution or
sickly nervous system, jump at once, without
any just process of reasoning, to the most
erroneous conclusions. I know as well as can
be that some of this description of my readers
will at once, without reflection, set my friend
down as a very rude ill-mannered sort of
person. Nothing of the kind, I assure you,
Miss. You never made a greater mistake in
your life. My friend was a highly respectable
person in his way; he was a great friend
and protector of rich, well-to-do pakehas;
he was, moreover, a great warrior, and had
killed the first man in several different
battles. He always wore, hanging round
his neck, a handsome carved flute, (this at
least showed a soft and musical turn of
mind,) which was made of the thigh-bone
of one of his enemies; and when Heke,

the Ngapuhi, made war against us, my friend came to the rescue, fought manfully for his pakeha friends, and was desperately wounded in so doing. Now can any one imagine a more respectable character ?—a warrior, a musician, a friend in need, who would stand by you while he had a leg to stand on, and would not eat a *friend* on any account whatever, except he should be very hungry.

The boat darts on ; she touches the edge of a steep rock ; the *"haere mai"* has subsided ; six or seven " personages"—the magnates of the tribe—come gravely to the front to meet me as I land. There is about six or seven yards of shallow water to be crossed between the boat and where they stand. A stout fellow rushes to the boat's nose, and "shows a back," as we used to say at leap-frog. He is a young fellow of respectable standing in the tribe, a far-off cousin of the chief's, a warrior, and as such has no back ; that is to say, to carry loads of fuel or potatos. He is too good a man to be spoiled in that way ; the women must carry for him ; the able-bodied men of the tribe must be saved for its protection ; but he is ready to carry the pakeha on shore—the *rangatira pakeha*, who wears a real *koti roa*, (a long coat,) and beaver hat! Carry! He would lie down and make a bridge of his body, with pleasure, for him. Has he not half a ship full of *taonga*?

Well, having stepped in as dignified a manner as I knew how, from thwart to thwart, till I came to the bow of the boat, and having tightened on my hat and buttoned up my coat, I fairly mounted on the broad shoulders of my aboriginal friend. I felt at the time that the thing was a sort of failure—a come down; the position was not graceful, or in any way likely to suggest ideas of respect or awe, with my legs projecting a yard or so from under each arm of my bearer, holding on to his shoulders in the most painful, cramped, and awkward manner. To be sacked on shore thus, and delivered like a bag of goods thus, into the hands of the assembled multitude, did not strike me as a good first appearance on this stage. But little, indeed, can we tell in this world what one second may produce. Gentle reader, fair reader, patient reader! The fates have decreed it; the fiat has gone forth; on that man's back I shall never land in New Zealand. Manifold are the doubts and fears which have yet to shake and agitate the hearts and minds of all my friends as to whether I shall ever land at all, or ever again feel *terra firma* touch my longing foot. My bearer made one step; the rock is slippery; backwards he goes; back, back! The steep is near—is passed! down, down, we go! backwards and headlong to the depths below!

The ebb tide is running like a sluice; in an instant we are forty yards off, and a fathom below the surface; ten more fathoms are beneath us. The heels of my boots, my polished boots, point to the upper air—aye, point; but when, oh, when again, shall I salute thee, gentle air; when again, unchoked by the saline flood, cry *Veni aura?* When, indeed! for now I am wrong end uppermost, drifting away with the tide, and ballasted with heavy pistols, boots, tight clothes, and all the straps and strings of civilisation. Oh, heavens! and oh earth! and oh ye little thieves of fishes who manage to live in the waters under the earth (a miserable sort of life you must have of it)! oh Maori sea nymphs! who, with yellow hair—yellow? egad—that's odd enough, to say the least of it; however the Maori should come to give their sea nymphs or spirits yellow hair is curious. The Maori know nothing about yellow hair ; their hair is black. About one in a hundred of them have a sort of dirty brown hair ; but even if there should be now and then a native with yellow hair, how is it that they have come to give this colour to the sea-sprites in particular ?—who also "dance on the sands, and yet no footstep seen." Now I confess I am rather puzzled and struck by the coincidence. I don't believe Shakespeare ever was in New Zealand ; Jasan might, being a sea-faring-man, and if he should have called in for wood and water, and happened to have the golden fleece by any accident on board, and by any chance put it on for a wig, why the thing would be accounted for at once. The world is mad now-a-days about gold, so no one cares a fig about what is called "golden hair ;" nuggets and dust have the preference ; but this is a grand mistake. Gold is no use, or very little, except in so far as this—that through the foolishness of human beings, one can purchase the necessaries and conveniences of life with it. Now, this being the case, if I have a chest full of gold (which I have not), I am no richer for it in fact until I have given it away in exchange for necessaries, comforts, and luxuries, which are, properly speaking, riches or wealth; but it follows from this, that he who has given me this same riches or wealth for my gold, has become poor, and his only chance to set himself up again, is to get rid of the gold as fast as he can, in exchange for the same sort and quantity of things, if he can get them, which is always doubtful. But here lies the gist of the matter—how did I, in the first instance, become possessed of my gold? If I bought it, and gave real wealth for it, beef, mutton, silk, tea, sugar, tobacco, ostrich feathers, leather breeches, and crinoline,—why, then, all I have done in parting with my gold, is merely to get them back again, and I am, consequently, no richer by the transaction; but if I steal my gold, then I am a clear gainer of the whole lot of valuables above mentioned. So, upon the whole, I don't see much use in getting gold honestly, and one must not steal it : digging it certainly is almost as good as stealing, if it is not too deep, which fully accounts for so many employing themselves in this way ; but then the same amount of labour would raise no end of wheat and potatoes, beef and mutton : and all farmers, mathematicians, and algebraists will agree

with me in this—that after any country is
fully cultivated, all the gold in the world
won't force it to grow one extra turnip, and
what more can any one desire ? So now Adam
Smith, McCulloch, and all the rest of them
may go and be hanged. The whole upshot of
this treatise on political economy and golden
hair, (which I humbly lay at the feet of the
Colonial Treasurer,) is this:—I would not
give one of your golden locks, my dear, for
all the gold, silver, pearls, diamonds, *mere
ponamus*—stop, let me think,—a good *mere
ponamu* would be a temptation. I had once
a *mere*, a present from a Maori friend, the
most beautiful thing of the kind ever seen.
It was nearly as transparent as glass ; in it
there were beautiful marks like fern leaves,
trees, fishes, and—I would not give much for
a person who could not see almost *anything* in
it. Never shall I cease to regret having
parted with it. The Emperor of Brazil, I
think, has it now ; but he does not know the
proper use of it. It went to the Minister many
years ago. I did not sell it. I would have
scorned to do that ; but I did expect to be
made knight of the golden pig knife, or
elephant and watch box, or something of that
nature : but here I am still, a mere pakeha

Maori, and, as I recollect, in desperate danger
of being drowned.

Up we came at last, blowing and puffing
like grampuses. With a glance I "recognised
the situation :"—we had drifted a long way
from the landing place. My hat was dashing
away before the land breeze towards the sea
and had already made a good "offing."
Three of the boat's-crew had jumped over-
board, had passed us a long distance, and
were seemingly bound after the hat; the
fourth man was pulling madly with one oar,
and consequently making great progress in
no very particular direction. The whole
tribe of natives had followed our drift along
the shore, shouting and gesticulating, and
some were launching a large canoe, evidently
bent on saving the *hat*, on which all eyes
were turned. As for the pakeha, it appears
they must have thought it an insult to his
understanding to suppose he could be
drowned anywhere in sight of land. " 'Did
he not come from the sea ? ' Was he not
a fish ? Was not the sea solid land to
him ? Did not his fire burn on the ocean ?
Had he not slept on the crests of the
waves ?" All this I heard afterwards ; but
at the time had I not been as much at home

in the water as anything not amphibious
could be, I should have been very little
better than a gone pakeha.   Here was a
pretty wind up!   I was going to "astonish
the natives," was I ?—with my black hat
and my *koti roa?*   But the villian is within a
yard of me—the rascally cause of all my grief.
The furies take possession of me ! I dart upon
him like a hungry shark! I have him! I
have him under ! Down, villain ! down to
the kraken and the whale, to the Taniwha
cave !—down ! down ! down !   As we sank
I heard one grand roar of wild laughter
from the shore—the word *utu* I heard roared
by many voices, but did not then know its
import.   The pakeha was drowning the
Maori for *utu* for himself, in *case* he should
be drowned.   No matter, if the Maori can't
hold his own, it's fair play ; and then, if the
pakeha really does drown the Maori, has
he not lots of *taonga* to be robbed of ?—no,
not exactly to be robbed of, either ; let us
not use unnecessarily bad language—we will
say to be distrained upon.   Crack ! What
do I hear ?   Down in the deep I felt a
shock, and actually heard a sudden noise.
Is it the "crack of doom ?"   No, it is
my frock-coat gone at one split "from clue

to caring"—split down the back. Oh if my pistols would go off, a fiery and watery death shouldst thou die, Caliban. Egad! they have gone off—they are both gone to the bottom! My boots are getting heavy! Humane Society, ahoy! where is your boat-hook?—where is your bellows? Humane Society, ahoy! We are now drifting fast by a sandy point, after which there will be no chance of landing,—the tide will take us right out to sea. My friend is very hard to drown —must finish him some other time. We both swim for the point, and land; and this is how I got ashore on Maori land.

CHAPTER III.

SOMETHING between a cheer, a scream, and a
roar, greet our arrival on the sand. An
English voice salutes me with "Well, you
served that fellow out." One half of my
coat hangs from my right elbow the other
from my left; a small shred of the collar is
still around my neck. My hat, alas! my hat
is gone. I am surrounded by a dense mob of
natives, laughing, shouting, and gesticulating,
in the most grotesque manner. Three
Englishmen are also in the crowd—they
seem greatly amused at something, and offer
repeated welcomes. At this moment up

comes my salt-water acquaintance, elbowing
his way through the crowd; there is a
strange serio-comic expression of anger in
his face; he stoops, makes horrid grimaces,
quivering at the same time his left hand and
arm about in a most extraordinary manner,
and striking the thick part of his left arm
with the palm of his right hand. "*Hu!*" says
he, "*hu! hu!*" "What *can* he mean?" said I.
"He is challenging you to wrestle," cried one
of the Englishmen; "he wants *utu*." "What
is *utu*?" said I. "Payment." "I won't pay
him." "Oh, that's not it, he wants to take
it out of you wrestling." "Oh, I see; here's
at him; pull off my coat and boots; I'll
wrestle him; his foot is in his own country,
and his name is—what?" "Sir, his name
in English means 'An eater of melons;' he
is a good wrestler; you must mind." "*Water-*
melons, I suppose; beef against melons for
ever, hurrah! here's at him." Here the natives began to run between us to separate us,
but seeing that I was in the humour to
"have it out," and that neither self or friend
were actually out of temper, and no doubt,
expecting to see the pakeha floored, they
stood to one side and made a ring. A
wrestler soon recognises another, and my

friend soon gave me some hints that showed
me I had some work before me. I was a
youngster in those days, all bone and sinew,
full of animal spirits, and as tough as leather.
A couple of desperate main strength efforts
soon convinced us both that science or endur-
ance must decide the contest. My antagonist
was a strapping fellow of about five-and-
twenty, tremendously strong, and much
heavier than me. I, however, in those days
actually could not be fatigued; I did not
know the sensation, and could run from
morning till night. I therefore trusted to
wearing him out, and avoiding his *ta* and
wiri. All this time the mob were shouting
encouragement to one or other of us. Such
a row never was seen. I soon perceived I
had a "party." "Well done, pakeha!"
"Now for it, Melons!" "At him again!"
"Take care, the pakeha is a *taniwha;* the
pakeha is a *tino tangata!*" "Hooray!"
(from the British element). "The Pakeha
is down!" "No he isn't!" (from English
side). Here I saw my friend's knees beginning to tremble. I made a great effort,
administered my favorite remedy, and there
lay the "Eater of melons" prone upon the
sand. I stood a victor; and like many other

conquerors, a very great loser. There I stood, *minus* hat, coat, and pistols, wet and mauled, and transformed very considerably for the worse since I left the ship. When my antagonist fell, the natives gave a great shout of triumph, and congratulated me in their own way with the greatest good will. I could see I had got their good opinion, though I scarcely could understand how. After sitting on the sand some time my friend arose, and with a very graceful movement, and a smile of good nature on his dusky countenance, he held out his hand and said in English, " How do you do ? "

I was much pleased at this ; the natives had given me fair play, and my antagonist, though defeated both by sea and land, offered me his hand, and welcomed me to the shore with his whole stock of English—" How do you do ? "

· But the row is not half over yet. Here comes the chief in the ship's boat. The other is miles off with its one man crew still pulling no one knows, or at all cares, where. Some one has been off in a canoe and told the chief that " Melons " and the " New Pakeha " were fighting like mad on the beach. Here he comes, flourishing his *mere ponamu*. He is a tall, stout fellow, in the prime of life, black

D

with tattooing, and splendidly dressed, according to the splendour of those days. He has on a very good blue jacket, no shirt or waistcoat, a pair of duck trousers, and a red sash round his waist; no hat or shoes, these being as yet things beyond a chief's ambition. The jacket was the only one in the tribe; and amongst the surrounding company I saw only one other pair of trousers, and it had a large hole at each knee, but this was not considered to detract at all from its value. The chief jumps ashore; he begins his oration, or rather to "blow up" all and sundry the tribe in general, and poor "Melons" in particular. He is really vexed, and wishes to appear to me more vexed than he really is. He runs, gesticulating and flourishing his *mere*, about ten steps in one direction, in the course of which ten steps he delivers a sentence; he then turns and runs back the same distance, giving vent to his wrath in another sentence, and so back and forward, forward and back, till he has exhausted the subject and tired his legs. The Englishmen were beside me and gave a running translation of what he said. "Pretty work this," he began, "*good* work; killing my pakeha; look at him! (Here a flourish in my direction with the *mere*.) I won't stand this; not at all! not at all! not at all! (The last sentence took three jumps, a step, and a turn-round, to keep correct time.) Who killed the pakeha? It was Melons. You are a nice man, are you not? (This with a sneer.) Killing my pakeha! (In a voice like thunder, and rushing savagely, *mere* in hand, at poor Melons, but turning exactly at the end of the ten steps and coming back again.) It will be heard of all over the country; we shall be called the 'pakeha killers;' I shall be sick with shame; the pakeha will run away, and take all his *taonga* along with him. What if you had killed him dead, or broken his bones? his relations would be coming across the sea for *utu*. (Great sensation, and I try to look as though I would say 'of course they would.') What did I build this pa close to the sea for?—was it not to trade with the pakehas?—and here you are killing the second that has come to stop with me. (Here poor Melons burst out crying like an infant.) Where is the hat?—where the *koti roa*?—where the shoes?—(Boots were shoes in those days.) The pakeha is robbed; he is murdered! (Here a howl from Melons, and I go over and sit down by him, clap

him on the bare back, and shake his hand.)
Look at that,—the pakeha does not bear
malice ; I would kill you if he asked me ;
you are a bad people, killers of pakehas ; be
off with you, the whole of you, away ! " This
command was instantly obeyed by all the
women, boys, and slaves. Melons also,
being in disgrace, disappeared ; but I
observed that "the whole of you" did not
seem to be understood as including the stout,
able-bodied, tattooed part of the population,
the strength of the tribe—the warriors, in
fact, many of whom counted themselves to
be very much about as good as the chief.
They were his nearest relations, without
whose support he could do nothing, and
were entirely beyond his control.

I found afterwards that it was only during
actual war that this chief was perfectly abso-
lute, which arose from the confidence the
tribe had in him, both as a general and a
fighting man, and the obvious necessity that
in war implicit obedience be given to one
head. I have, however, observed in other
tribes, that in war they would elect a chief
for the occasion, a war chief, and have been
surprised to see the obedience they gave him,
even when his conduct was very open to ·

criticism. I say with surprise, for the natives
are so self-possessed, opinionated, and repub-
lican, that the chiefs have at ordinary times
but little control over them, except in very
rare cases, where the chief happens to possess
a singular vigour of character, or some other
unusual advantage, to enable him to keep
them under.

I will mention here that my first antagonist,
"The Eater of Melons," became a great friend
of mine. He was my right-hand man and
manager when I set up house on my own
account, and did me many friendly services in
the course of my acquaintance with him. He
came to an unfortunate end some years later.
The tribe were getting ready for a war expedition; poor Melons was filling cartridges
from a fifty pound barrel of gunpowder, pouring the gunpowder into the cartridges with
his hand, and smoking his pipe at the time,
as I have seen the natives doing fifty times
since. A spark fell into the cask, and it is
scarcely necessary to say that my poor friend
was roasted alive in a second. I have known
three other accidents of the same kind, from
smoking whilst filling cartridges. In one of
these accidents three lives were lost, and
many injured; and I really do believe that

the certainty of death will not prevent some
of the natives from smoking for more than a
given time. I have often seen infants refuse
the mother's breast, and cry for the pipe till
it was given them ; and dying natives often
ask for a pipe, and die smoking. I can
clearly perceive that the young men of the
present day are neither so tall, or stout, or
strong as men of the same age were when I
first came to the country ; and I believe that
this smoking from their infancy is one of the
chief causes of this decrease in strength and
stature.

I am landed at last, certainly ; but I am
tattered and wet, and in a most deplorable
plight : so to make my story short, for I see,
if I am too particular, I shall never come to
the end of it, I returned to the ship, put
myself to rights, and came on shore next day
with all my *taonga*, to the great delight of
the chief and tribe. My hospitable enter-
tainer, Mr. —, found room for my possessions
in his store, and a room for myself in his
house ; and so now I am fairly housed we
shall see what will come of it.

I have now all New Zealand before me to
caper about in ; so I shall do as I like, and
please myself. I shall keep to neither rule,

rhyme, or reason, but just write what comes uppermost to my recollection of the good old days. Many matters which seemed odd enough to me at first, have long appeared such mere matters of course, that I am likely to pass them over without notice. I shall, however, give some of the more striking features of those delectable days, now, alas! passed and gone. Some short time after this, news came that a grand war expedition, which had been absent nearly two years at the South, had returned. This party were about a thousand strong, being composed of two parties of about five hundred men each, from two different tribes, who had joined their force for the purpose of the expedition. The tribe with which Mr. — and myself were staying, had not sent any men on this war party; but, I suppose to keep their hands in, had attacked one of the two tribes who had, and who were, consequently, much weakened by the absence of so many of their best men. It, however, turned out that after a battle —the ferocity of which has seldom been equalled in any country but this—our friends were defeated with a dreadful loss, having inflicted almost as great on the enemy. Peace, however, had afterwards been formally made;

but, nevertheless, the news of the return of this expedition was not heard without causing a sensation almost amounting to consternation. The war chief of the party who had been attacked by our friends during his absence, was now, with all his men, within an easy day's march. His road lay right through our village, and it was much to be doubted that he would keep the peace, being one of the most noted war chiefs of New Zealand, and he and his men returning from a successful expedition. All now was uproar and confusion; messengers were running like mad, in all directions, to call in stragglers; the women were carrying fuel and provisions into the pa or fortress of the tribe. This pa was a very well built and strong stockade, composed of three lines of strong fence and ditch, very ingeniously and artificially planned; and, indeed, as good a defence as well could be imagined against an enemy armed only with musketry.

All the men were now working like furies, putting this fort to rights, getting it into fighting order, mending the fences, clearing out the ditches, knocking down houses inside the place, clearing away brushwood and fern all around the outside within musket shot.

I was in the thick of it, and worked all day lashing the fence ; the fence being of course not nailed, but lashed with *toro-toro*, a kind of tough creeping plant, like a small rope, which was very strong and well adapted for the purpose. This lashing was about ten or twelve feet from the ground, and a stage had to be erected for the men to stand on. To accomplish this lashing or fastening of the fence well and with expedition required two men, one inside the fence and another outside ; all the men therefore worked in pairs, passing the end of the *toro-toro* from one to the other through the fence of large upright stakes and round a cross piece which went all along the fence, by which means the whole was connected into one strong wall. I worked away like fury, just as if I had been born and bred a member of the community ; and moreover, not being in those days very particularly famous for what is called prudence, I intended also, circumstances permitting, to fight like fury too, just for the fun of the thing. About a hundred men were employed in this part of the work now lashing the pa. My *vis-à-vis* in the operation was a respectable old warrior of great experience and approved valour, whose name being turned into English meant

"The eater of his own relations." (Be careful not to read *rations*.) This was quite a different sort of diet from "melons," and he did not bear his name for nothing, as I could tell you if I had time, but I am half mad with haste lashing the pa. I will only say that my comrade was a most bloodthirsty, ferocious, athletic savage, and his character was depicted in every line of his tattooed face. About twenty men had been sent out to watch the approach of the dreaded visitors. The repairing of the stockade went on all one day and all one night by torchlight and by the light of huge fires lit in the inside. No one thought of sleep. Dogs barking, men shouting, children crying, women screaming, pigs squealing, muskets firing (to see if they were fit for active service and would go off), and above all the doleful *tetere* sounding. This was a huge wooden trumpet six feet long, which gave forth a groaning moaning sound, like the voice of a dying wild bull. Babel, with a dash of Pandemonium, will give a faint idea of the uproar.

All preparations having been at last made, and no further tidings of the enemy, as I may call them, I took a complete survey of the fort, my friend the "Relation Eater" being my

companion and explaining to me the design
of the whole. I learned something that day;
and I, though pretty well "up" in the noble
science of fortification, ancient and modern,
was obliged to confess to myself that a savage
who could neither read or write—who had
never heard of Cohorn or Vauban—and who
was moreover avowedly a gobbler up of his
own relations, could teach me certain practical
"dodges" in the defensive art quite well
worth knowing.

A long shed of palm leaves had been also
built at a safe and convenient distance from
the fort. This was for the accommodation of
the expected visitors, supposing they came in
peaceful guise. A whole herd of pigs were
also collected and tied to stakes driven into
the ground in the rear of the fort. These were
intended to feast the coming guests, according
to their behaviour.

Towards evening a messenger from a
neighbouring friendly tribe arrived to say
that next day, about noon, the strangers
might be expected; and also that the peace
which had been concluded with their tribe
during their absence, had been ratified and
accepted by them. This was satisfactory
intelligence; but, nevertheless, no precaution

must be neglected. To be thrown off guard would invite an attack, and ensure destruction ; everything must be in order ; gun cleaning, flint fixing, cartridge making, was going on in all directions ; and the outpost at the edge of the forest was not called in. All was active preparation.

The path by which these doubtful friends were coming led through a dense forest and came out on the clear plain about half-a-mile from the pa, which plain continued and extended in every direction around the fortress to about the same distance, so that none could approach unperceived. The outpost of twenty men were stationed at about a couple of hundred yards from the point where the path emerged from the wood ; and as the ground sloped considerably from the forest to the fort, the whole intervening space was clearly visible.

Another night of alarm and sleepless expectation, the melancholy moan of the *tetere* still continuing to hint to any lurking enemy that we were all wide awake ; or rather, I should say, to assure him most positively of it, for who could sleep with that diabolical din in his ears ? Morning came and an early breakfast was cooked and devoured hurriedly.

Then groups of the younger men might be
seen here and there fully armed, and "getting
up steam" by dancing the war dance, in antici-
pation of the grand dance of the whole warrior
force of the tribe, which, as a matter of course,
must be performed in honour of the visitors
when they arrived.   In honour, but quite as
much in intimidation, or an endeavour at it,
though no one said so.   Noon arrived at last.
Anxious glances are turning from all quarters
towards the wood, from which a path is plainly
seen winding down the sloping ground towards
the pa.   The outpost is on the alert.   Straggling
scouts are out in every direction.   All is expectation.   Now there is a movement at the
outpost.   They suddenly spread in an open
line, ten yards between each man.   One man
comes at full speed running towards the pa,
jumping and bounding over every impedi-
ment.   Now something moves in the border
of the forest,—it is a mass of black heads.
Now the men are plainly visible.   The whole
taua has emerged upon the plain.   "Here
they come ! here they come !" is heard in all
directions.   The men of the outpost cross the ·
line of march in pretended resistance ; they
present their guns, make horrid grimaces,
dance about like mad baboons, and then fall

back with headlong speed to the next ad-
vantageous position for making a stand.   The
taua, however, comes on steadily ; they are
formed in a solid oblong mass.   The chief at
the left of the column leads them on.   The
men are all equipped for immediate action,
that is to say, quite naked except their arms
and cartridge boxes, which are a warrior's
clothes.   No one can possibly tell what this
peaceful meeting may end in, so all are
ready for action at a second's notice.   The
taua still comes steadily on.   As I have said,
the men are all stripped for action, but I
also notice that the appearance of nakedness
is completely taken away by the tattooing,
the colour of the skin, and the arms and
equipments.   The men in fact look much
better than when dressed in their Maori
clothing.   Every man, almost without exception, is covered with tattooing from the
knees to the waist ; the face is also covered
with dark spiral lines.   Each man has round
his middle a belt, to which is fastened two
cartridge boxes, one behind and one before ;
. another belt goes over the right shoulder and
under the left arm, and from it hangs, on the
left side and rather behind, another cartridge
box, and under the waist-belt is thrust,

behind, at the small of the back, the short-handled tomahawk for close fight and to finish the wounded. Each cartridge box contains eighteen rounds, and every man has a musket. Altogether this *taua* is better and more uniformly armed and equipped than ordinary; but they have been amongst the first who got pakehas to trade with them, and are indeed in consequence the terror of New Zealand. On they come, a set of tall, athletic, heavy-made men; they would, I am sure, in the aggregate weigh some tons heavier than the same number of men taken at random from the streets of one of our manufacturing towns. They are now half way across the plain; they keep their formation, a solid oblong, admirably as they advance, but they do not keep step; this causes a very singular appearance at a distance. Instead of the regular marching step of civilised soldiers, which may be observed at any distance, this mass seems to progress towards you with the creeping motion of some great reptile at a distance, and when coming down a sloping ground this effect is quite remarkable.

The mimic opposition is now discontinued; the outpost rushes in at full speed, the men firing their guns in the air as they run. *Takini! takini!* is the cry, and out spring three young men, the best runners of our tribe, to perform the ceremony of the *taki*. They hold in their hands some reeds to represent darts or *kokiri*. At this moment a tremendous fire of *ball* cartridge opens from the fort; the balls whistle in every direction, over and around the advancing party, who steadily and gravely come on, not seeming to know that a gun has been fired, though they perfectly well understand that this salute is also a hint of full prepartion for any unexpected turn things may take. Now, from the whole female population arises the shrill *"haere mai! haere mai!"* Mats are waving, guns firing, dogs barking; the chief roaring to " fall in," and form for the war dance. He appears half mad with excitement, anxiety, and something very like apprehension of a sudden onslaught from his friends. In the midst of this horrible uproar off dart three runners. They are not unexpected. Three young men of the *taua* are seen to tighten their waist belts, and hand their muskets to their comrades. On go the three young men from the fort. They approach the front of the advancing column; they dance and caper about like

mad monkeys, twisting their faces about in
the most extraordinary manner, shewing the
whites of their eyes, and lolling out their
tongues. At last, after several feints, they
boldly advance within twenty yards of the
supposed enemy, and send the reed darts
flying full in their faces : then they turn and
fly as if for life. Instantly, from the stranger
ranks, three young men dart forth in eager
pursuit; and behind them comes the solid
column, rushing on at full speed. Run now,
O "Sounding Sea," *(Tai Haruru)* for the
"Black Cloud," *(Kapua Manga)* the swiftest
of the Rarawa, is at your back ; run now, for
the honour of your tribe and your own name,
run! run! It was an exciting scene. The
two famous runners came on at a tremendous
pace, the dark mass of armed men following
close behind at full speed, keeping their formation admirably, the ground shaking under
them as they rushed on. On come the two
runners (the others are left behind and dis-
regarded). The pursuer gains upon his man ;
but they are fast nearing the goal, where,
according to Maori custom, the chase must
end. Run, " Sounding Sea ;" another effort !
your tribe are near in full array, and armed
for the war dance ; their friendly ranks are

E

your refuge ; run ! run !   On came the headlong race.   When within about thirty yards of
the place where our tribe was now formed
in a solid oblong, each man kneeling on one
knee, with musket held in both hands, butt to
ground, and somewhat sloped to the front,
the pursuing native caught at the shoulder
of our man, touched it, but could do no more.
Here he must stop ;· to go farther would not
be "correct."   He will, however, boast every-
where that he has touched the shoulder of
the famous " Sounding Sea."   Our man has
not, however, been caught, which would have
been a bad omen.   At this moment the
charging column comes thundering up to
where their man is standing ; instantly they
all kneel upon one knee, holding their guns
sloped before their faces, in the manner
already described.   The *elite* of the two tribes
are now opposite to each other, all armed,
all kneeling, and formed in two solid oblong
masses, the narrow end of the oblong to the
front.   Only thirty yards divide them ; the
front ranks do not gaze on each other ; both
parties turn their eyes towards the ground,
and with heads bent downwards, and a little
to one side, appear to listen.   All is silence ;
you might have heard a pin drop.   The

uproar has turned to a calm; the men are kneeling statues; the chiefs have disappeared; they are in the centre of their tribes. The pakeha is beginning to wonder what will be the end of all this; and also to speculate on the efficacy of the buck shot with which his gun is loaded, and wishes it was ball. Two minutes have elapsed in this solemn silence, the more remarkable as being the first quiet two minutes for the last two days and nights. Suddenly from the extreme rear of the strangers' column is heard a scream—a horrid yell. A savage, of herculean stature, comes, *mere* in hand, and rushing madly to the front. He seems hunted by all the furies. Bedlam never produced so horrid a visage. Thrice, as he advances, he gives that horrid cry; and thrice the armed tribe give answer with a long-drawn gasping sigh. He is at the front; he jumps into the air, shaking his stone weapon; the whites only of his eyes are visible, giving a most hideous appearance to his face; he shouts the first words of the war song, and instantly his tribe spring from the ground. It would be hard to describe the scene which followed. The roaring chorus of the war song; the horrid grimaces; the eyes

all white ; the tongues hanging out ; the
furious yet measured and uniform gesticu-
lation, jumping, and stamping. I felt the
ground plainly trembling. At last the war
dance ended ; and then my tribe, (I find I
am already beginning to get Maorified,)
starting from the ground like a single man,
endeavoured to out-do even their amiable
friends' exhibition. They end ; then the new-
comers perform another demon dance ; then
my tribe give another. Silence again prevails, and all sit down. Immediately a man
from the new arrivals comes to the front of
his own party ; he runs to and fro ; he speaks
for his tribe ; these are his words :—" Peace
is made ! peace is made ! peace is firm ! peace
is secure ! peace ! peace ! peace ! " This man
is not a person of any particular consequence
in his tribe, but his brother was killed by our
people in the battle I have mentioned, and
this gives him the right to be the first to
proclaim peace. His speech is ended and he
" falls in." Some three or four others
" follow on the same side." Their speeches
are short also, and nearly verbatim what the
first was. Then who of all the world starts
forth from " ours," to speak on the side of
" law and order," but my diabolical old

acquaintance the "Relation Eater." I had
by this time picked up a little Maori, and
could partly understand his speech. "Welcome! welcome! welcome! peace is made!
not till now has there been true peace! I
have seen you, and peace is made!" Here
he broke out into a song, the chorus of which
was taken up by hundreds of voices, and
when it ended he made a sudden and very
expressive gesture of scattering something
with his hands, which was a signal to all
present that the ceremonial was at an end for
the time. Our tribe at once disappeared into
the pa, and at the same instant the strangers
broke into a scattered mob, and made for the
long shed which had been prepared for their
reception, which was quite large enough, and
the floor covered thickly with clean rushes to
sleep on. About fifty or sixty then started
for the border of the forest to bring their
clothes and baggage, which had been left
there as incumbrances to the movements of
the performers in the ceremonials I have
described. Part, however, of the "*impedi-
menta*" had already arrived on the backs
of about thirty boys, women, and old
slaves; and I noticed amongst other things
some casks of cartridges, which were, as

I thought, rather ostentatiously exposed to view.

I soon found the reason my friend of saturnine propensities had closed proceedings so abruptly was, that the tribe had many pressing duties of hospitality to fulfil, and that the heavy talking was to commence next day. I noticed also that to this time there had been no meeting of the chiefs, and, more-over, that the two parties had kept strictly separate—the nearest they had been to each other was thirty yards when the war dancing was going on, and they seemed quite glad, when the short speeches were over, to move off to a greater distance from each other.

Soon after the dispersion of the two parties, a firing of muskets was heard in and at the rear of the fort, accompanied by the squeaking, squealing, and dying groans of a whole herd of pigs. Directly afterwards a mob of fellows were seen staggering under the weight of the dead pigs, and proceeding to the long shed already mentioned, in front of which they were flung down, *sans-cere-monie*, and without a word spoken. I counted sixty-nine large fat pigs flung in one heap, one on the top of the other, before that part of the shed where the

principal chief was sitting; twelve were
thrown before the interesting savage who
had "started" the war dance ; and several
single porkers were thrown without any
remark before certain others of the guests.
The parties, however, to whom this compliment was paid sat quietly saying nothing,
and hardly appearing to see what was done.
Behind the pigs was placed, by the active
exertion of two or three hundred people, a
heap of potatoes and *kumera*, in quantity
about ten tons, so there was no want of the
raw material for a feast.

The pigs and potatoes having been deposited, a train of women appeared—the
whole, indeed, of the young and middle-aged
women of the tribe, They advanced with a
half-dancing half-hopping sort of step, to the
time of a wild but not unmusical chant,
each woman holding high in both hands a
smoking dish of some kind or other of Maori
delicacy, hot from the oven. The ground-
work of this feast appeared to be sweet
potatoes and *taro*, but on the top of each
smoking mess was placed either dried shark,
eels, mullet, or pork, all "piping hot." This
treat was intended to stay our guests'
stomachs till they could find time to cook

for themselves. The women having placed the dishes, or to speak more correctly, baskets, on the ground before the shed, disappeared ; and in a miraculously short time the feast disappeared also, as was proved by seeing the baskets flung in twos, threes, and tens, empty out of the shed.

Next day, pretty early in the morning, I saw our chief, (as I must call him for distinction) with a few of the principal men of the tribe, dressed in their best Maori costume, taking their way towards the shed of the visitors. When they got pretty near, a cry of *haere mai!* hailed them. They went on gravely, and observing where the principal chief was seated, our chief advanced towards him, fell upon his neck embracing him in the most affectionate manner, commenced a *tangi*, or melancholy sort of ditty, which lasted a full half hour, and during which, both parties, as in duty bound and in compliance with custom, shed floods of tears. How they managed to do it is more than I can tell to this day, except that I suppose you may train a man to do anything. Right well do I know that either party would have almost given his life for a chance to exterminate the other with all his tribe ; and twenty-seven

years afterwards I saw the two tribes fighting
in the very quarrel which was pretended to
have been made up that day. Before this,
however, both these chiefs were dead, and
others reigned in their stead. While the
tangi was going on between the two principals, the companions of our chief each
selected one of the visitors, and rushing into
his arms, went .through a similar scene. Old
"Relation Eater" singled out the horrific
savage who had began the war dance, and
these two tender-hearted individuals did, for a
full half hour, seated on the ground, hanging
on each other's necks, give vent to such a
chorus of skilfully modulated howling as would
have given Momus the blue devils to listen to.

After the *tangi* was ended, the two tribes
seated themselves in a large irregular circle
on the plain, and into this circle strode an
orator, who, having said his say, was followed
by another, and so the greater part of the day
was consumed. No arms were to be seen in
the hands of either party, except the greenstone *mere* of the principal chiefs ; but I took
notice that about thirty of our people never
left the nearest gate of the pa, and that their
loaded muskets, although out of sight, were
close at hand, standing against the fence

inside the gate, and I also perceived that under their cloaks or mats they wore their cartridge boxes and tomahawks. This caused me to observe the other party more closely. They also, I perceived, had some forty men sleeping in the shed ; these fellows had not removed their cartridge boxes either, and all their companions' arms were carefully ranged behind them in a row, six or seven deep, against the back wall of the shed.

The speeches of the orators were not very interesting, so I took a stroll to a little rising ground at about a hundred yards distance, where a company of natives, better dressed than common, were seated. They had the best sort of ornamented cloaks, and had feathers in their heads, which I already knew "commoners" could not afford to wear, as they were only to be procured some hundreds of miles to the south. I therefore concluded these were magnates or "personages" of some kind or other, and determined to introduce myself. As I approached, one of these splendid individuals nodded to me in a very familiar sort of manner, and I, not to appear rude, returned the salute. I stepped into the circle formed by my new friends, and had just commenced a *tena koutou*, when a breeze of wind came sighing along the hill-top. My friend nodded again,—his cloak blew to one side. What do I see?—or rather what do I not see? *The head has no body under it!* The heads had all been stuck on slender rods, a cross stick tied on to represent the shoulders, and the cloaks thrown over all in such a natural man- ner as to deceive anyone at a short distance, but a green pakeha, who was not expecting any such matter, to a certainty. I fell back a yard or two, so as to take a full view of this silent circle. I began to feel as if at last I had fallen into strange company. I began to look more closely at my companions, and to try to fancy what their characters in life had been. One had undoubtedly been a warrior ; there was something bold and defiant about the whole air of the head. Another was the head of a very old man, grey, shrivelled, and wrinkled. I was going on with my observa- tions when I was saluted by a voice from behind with, " Looking at the eds, sir ?" It was one of the pakehas formerly mentioned. " Yes," said I, turning round just the least possible thing quicker than ordinary. " Eds has been a getting scarce," says he. " I should think so," says I. " We an't ad a ed this long time," says he. " The devil !" says

I. "One o' them eds has been hurt bad," says he. "I should think all were, rather so," says I. "Oh no, only one on 'em," says he, "the skull is split, and it won't fetch nothin," says he. "Oh, murder! I see, now," says I. "Eds was *werry* scarce," says he, shaking his own "ed." "Ah!" said I. "They had to tattoo a slave a bit ago," says he, "and the villain ran away, tattooin' and all!" says he. "What?" said I. "Bolted afore he was fit to kill," says he. "Stole off with his own head?" says I. "That's just it," says he. "*Capital* felony!" says I. "You may say that, sir," says he. "Good morning," said I. I walked away pretty smartly. "Loose notions about heads in this country," said I to myself; and involuntarily putting up my hand to my own, I thought somehow the bump of combativeness felt smaller, or indeed had vanished altogether. "It's all very funny," said I.

I walked down into the plain. I saw in one place a crowd of women, boys, and others. There was a great noise of lamentation going on. I went up to the crowd, and there beheld, lying on a clean mat, which was spread on the ground, another head. A number of women were standing in a row before it, screaming, wailing, and quivering their hands about in a most extraordinary manner, and cutting themselves dreadfully with sharp flints and shells. One old woman, in the centre of the group, was one clot of blood from head to feet, and large clots of coagulated blood lay on the ground where she stood. The sight was absolutely horrible, I thought at the time. She was singing or howling a dirge-like wail. In her right hand she held a piece of *tuhua*, or volcanic glass, as sharp as a razor : this she placed deliberately to her left wrist, drawing it slowly upwards to her left shoulder, the spouting blood following as it went ; then from the left shoulder downwards, across the breast to the short ribs on the right side ; then the rude but keen knife was shifted from the right hand to the left, placed to the right wrist, drawn upwards to the right shoulder, and so down across the breast to the left side, thus making a bloody cross on the breast ; and so the operation went on all the time I was there, the old creature all the time howling in time and measure, and keeping time also with the knife, which at every cut was shifted from one hand to the other, as I have described. She had scored her forehead and cheeks before I came ; her face and body was a mere clot of blood, and a little stream was dropping from every finger —a more hideous object could scarcely be conceived. I took notice that the younger women, though they screamed as loud, did not cut near so deep as the old woman, especially about the face.

This custom has been falling gradually out of use; and when practised now, in these degenerate times, the cutting and maiming is mere form, mere scratching to draw enough blood to swear by: but, in "the good old times," the thing used to be done properly. I often, of late years, have felt quite indignant to see some degenerate hussey making believe with a piece of flint in her hand, but who had no notion of cutting herself up properly as she ought to do. It shews a want of natural affection in the present generation, I think; they refuse to shed tears of blood for their friends as their mothers used to do.

This head, I found on enquiry, was not the head of an enemy. A small party of our friends had been surprised; two brothers were flying for their lives down a hill-side; a shot broke the leg of one of them and he fell; the enemy were close at hand; already the exulting cry " *na! na! mate raua!* " was heard ; the wounded man cried to the brother " Do not leave my head a plaything for the foe." There was no time for deliberation. The brother *did not* deliberate ; a few slashes with the tomahawk saved his brother's head, and he escaped with it in his hand, dried it, and brought it home ; and the old woman was the mother,—the young ones were cousins. There was no sister, as I heard, when I enquired. All the heads on the hill were heads of enemies, and several of them are now in museums in Europe.

With reference to the knowing remarks of the pakeha who accosted me on the hill on the state of the head market, I am bound to remark that my friend Mr. —— never speculated in this " article ;" but the skippers of many of the colonial trading schooners were always ready to deal with a man who had " a real good head," and used to commission such men as my companion of the morning to " pick up heads " for them. It is a positive fact that some time after this the head of a live man was sold and paid for beforehand, and afterwards honestly delivered " as per agreement. "

The scoundrel slave who had the conscience

to run away with his own head after the trouble and expense had been gone to to tattoo it to make it more valuable, is no fiction either. Even in "the good old times" people would sometimes be found to behave in the most dishonest manner. But there are good and bad to be found in all times and places.

Now if there is one thing I hate more than another it is the raw-head-and-bloody-bones style of writing, and in these random reminiscences I shall avoid all particular mention of battles, massacres, and onslaughts, except there be something particularly characteristic of my friend the Maori in them. As for mere hacking and hewing, there has been enough of that to be had in Europe, Asia, and America of late, and very well described too, by numerous "our correspondents." If I should have to fight a single combat or two, just to please the ladies, I shall do my best not to get killed, and hereby promise not to kill anyone myself if I possibly can help it. I, however, hope to be excused for the last two or three pages, as it was necessary to point out 'that in the good old times, if one's own head was not sufficient, it was quite practicable to get another.

I must, however, get rid of our visitors.
Next day, at daylight, they disappeared :
canoes from their own tribe had come to meet
them, (the old woman with the flint had arrived in these canoes,) and they departed *sans-
ceremonie*, taking with them all that was left
of the pigs and potatoes which had been
given them, and also the " fine lot of eds."
Their departure was felt as a great relief,
and though it was satisfactory to know peace
was made, it was even more so to be well rid
of the peacemakers.

Hail, lovely peace, daughter of heaven !
meek-eyed inventor of Armstrong guns and
Enfield rifles ; you of the liquid-fire-shell,
hail ! Shooter at " bulls'-eyes," trainer of
battalions, killer of wooden Frenchmen, hail !
(A bit of fine writing does one good.)
Nestling under thy wing, I will scrape sharp
the point of my spear with a *pipi* shell ; I
will carry fern-root into my pa ; I will *cure*
those heads which I have killed in war, or
they will spoil and " won't fetch nothin" : for
these are thy arts, O peace !

CHAPTER IV.

PAKEHAS, though precious in the good old
times, would sometimes get into awkward
scrapes. Accidents, I have observed, will happen at the best of times. Some time after the
matters I have been recounting happened,
two of the pakehas who were "knocking
about" Mr. —— premises, went fishing. One
of them was a very respectable old man-of-
war's man ; the other was the connoisseur of
heads, who, I may as well mention, was
thought to be one of that class who never
could remember to a nicety how they had
come into the country, or where they came
from. It so happened that on their return,
the little boat, not being well fastened, went
adrift in the night, and was cast on shore
at about four miles distance, in the dominions
of a petty chief who was a sort of vassal or

retainer of ours. He did not belong to the tribe, and lived on the land by the permission of our chief as a sort of tenant at will. Of late an ill-feeling had grown up between him and the principal chief. The vassal had in fact begun to show some airs of independence, and had collected more men about him than our chief cared to see ; but up to this time there had been no regular outbreak between them, possibly because the vassal had not yet sufficient force to declare independence formally. Our chief was however watching for an excuse to fall out with him before he should grow too strong. As soon as it was heard where the boat was, the two men went for it as a matter of course, little thinking that this encroaching vassal would have the insolence to claim the right of "flotsam and jetsam," which belonged to the principal chief, and which was always waived in favour of his pakehas. On arrival, however, at this rebellious chief's dominions, they were informed that it was his intention to stick to the boat until he was paid a "stocking of gunpowder"—meaning a quantity as much as a stocking would hold, which was the regular standard measure in those days in that locality. A stocking of gunpowder! who ever heard of such an awful imposition? The demand was enormous in value and rebellious in principle. The thing must be put an end to at once. The principal chief did not hesitate : rebellion must be crushed in the bud. He at once mustered his whole force, (he did not approve of "little wars,") and sent them off under the command of the Relation Eater, who served an ejectment in regular Maori form, by first plundering the village and then burning it to ashes ; also destroying the cultivation and provisions, and forcing the vassal to decamp with all his people on pain of instant massacre—a thing they did not lose a moment in doing, and I don't think they either eat or slept till they had got fifty miles off, where a tribe related to them received them and gave them a welcome.

Well, about three months after this, about daylight in the morning, I was aroused by a great uproar of men shouting, doors smashing, and women screaming. Up I jumped, and pulled on a few clothes in less time, I am sure, that ever I had done before in my life ; out I ran, and at once perceived that Mr. —— premises were being sacked by the rebellious vassal, who had returned with about fifty men, and was taking this means of revenging himself for the rough handling he had received from our chief. Men were rushing in mad haste through the smashed windows and doors, loaded with anything and everything they could lay hands on. The chief was stamping against the door of a room in which he was aware the most valuable goods were kept, and shouting for help to break it open. A large canoe was floating close to the house, and was being rapidly filled with plunder. I saw a fat old Maori woman, who was washer-woman to the establishment, being dragged along the ground by a huge fellow, who was trying to tear from her grasp one of my shirts, to which she clung with perfect desperation. I perceived at a glance that the faithful old creature would probably save a sleeve. A long line of similar articles, my property, which had graced the *taiepa* fence the night before, had disappeared. The old man-of-war's man had placed his back exactly oppo-site to that part of the said fence where hung a certain striped cotton shirt and well scrubbed canvas trowsers, which *could* belong to no one but himself. He was "hitting out" lustily right and left. Mr. —— had been absent some days on a journey, and the head merchant, as we found after all was over, was

hiding under a bed. When the old sailor
saw me, he "sang out," in a voice clear as a
bell, and calculated to be distinctly heard
above the din :—"Hit out, sir, if you please ;
let's make a fight of it the best we can ; our
mob will be here in five minutes ; Tahuna
has run to fetch them." While he thus gave
both advice and information, he also set a
good example, having delivered just one
thump per word or thereabouts. The odds
were terrible, but the time was short that I
was required to fight ; so I at once floored a
native who was rushing by me. He fell like
a man shot, and I then perceived he was one
of our own people who had been employed
about the place ; so, to balance things, I
knocked down another, and then felt myself
seized round the waist from behind, by a
fellow who seemed to be about as strong as a
horse. At this moment I cast an anxious
glance around the field of battle. The old
Maori woman had, as I expected, saved a
good half of my shirt ; she had got on the top
of an out-house, and was waving it in a
"Sister Anne" sort of manner, and calling
to an imaginary friendly host, which she pretended to see advancing to the rescue. The
old sailor had fallen under, but not sur-

rendered to, superior force. Three natives had got him down; but it took all they could do to *keep* him down : he was evidently carrying out his original idea of making a fight of it, and gaining time ;—the striped shirt and canvas trowsers still hung proudly on the fence. None of his assailants could spare a second to pull them down. I was kicking and flinging in the endeavour to extricate myself; or, at least to turn round, so as to carry out a "face to face" policy, which it would be a grand mistake to suppose was not understood long ago in the good old times. I had nearly succeeded, and was thinking what particular form of destruction I should shower on the foe, when a tremendous shout was heard. It was "our mob" coming to the rescue ; and, like heroes of old, " sending their voice before them." In an instant both myself and the gallant old tar were released ; the enemy dashed on board their canoe, and in another moment were off, darting away before a gale of wind and a fair tide at a rate that put half a mile at least between them and us before our protectors came up. " Load the gun !" cried the sailor—(there was a nine pound carronade on the cliff before the house, overlooking the river). A cartridge was soon found, and a shot, and the gun loaded. "Slew her a little," cried my now commander; "fetch a fire stick." "Aye, aye, sir" (from self). "Wait a little; that will do—Fire!"—(in a voice as if ordering the discharge of the whole broadside of a three-decker). Bang! The elevation was perfectly correct. The shot struck the water at exactly the right distance, and only a few feet to one side. A very few feet more to the right and the shot would have entered the stern of the canoe, and, as she was end on to us, would have killed half the people in her. A miss, however, is as good as a mile off. The canoe disappeared behind a point, and there we were with an army of armed friends around us, who, by making great expedition, had managed to come exactly in time to be too late.

This was a *taua muru* (a robbing expedition) in revenge for the leader having been cleaned out by our chief, which gave them the right to rob any one connected with, related to, or under the protection of, our chief aforesaid, provided always that they were able. We, on the other hand, had the clear right to kill any of the robbers, which would then have given them the right to kill us; but until we killed some of them, it would not have been "correct" for them to have taken life, so they managed the thing neatly, so that they should have no occasion to do so. The whole proceeding was un-objectionable in every respect, and *tika* (correct). Had we put in our nine-pound shot at the stern of their canoe, it would have been correct also, but as we were not able, we had no right whatever to complain.

The above is good law, and here I may as well inform the New Zealand public that I am going to write the whole law of this land in a book, which I shall call *"Ko nga ture;"* and as I intend it for the good of both races, I shall mix the two languages up in such a way that neither can understand; but this does not matter, as I shall add a "glossary," in Coptic, to make things clear.

Some time after this, a little incident happened at my friend Mr. —— place worth noting. Our chief had, for some time back, a sort of dispute with another magnate, who lived about ten miles off. I really cannot say who was in the right—the arguments on both sides were so nearly balanced, that I should not like to commit myself to a judg-ment in the case. The question was at last brought to a fair hearing at my friend's house. The arguments on both sides were very forcible, so much so that in the course of the arbitration our chief and thirty of his principal witnesses were shot dead in a heap before my friend's door, and sixty others badly wounded, and my friend's house and store blown up and burnt to ashes. My friend was all but, or indeed, quite ruined, but it would not have been "correct" for him to complain—*his* loss in goods being far over-balanced by the loss of the tribe in men. He was, however, consoled by hundreds of friends who came in large parties to condole and *tangi* with him, and who, as was quite correct in such cases, shot and eat all his stock, sheep, pigs, goats, ducks, geese, fowls, &c., all in high compliment to himself, at which he felt proud, as a well conducted and conditioned pakeha Maori (as he was) should do. He did not, however, survive these honours long, poor fellow. He died, and strange to say, no one knew exactly what was the matter with him—some said it was the climate, they thought.

After this the land about which this little misunderstanding had arisen, was, so to speak, thrown into chancery, where it has now remained about forty years; but I hear that proceedings are to commence *de novo* (no allusion to the " new system ") next summer, or at farthest the summer after ; and as I witnessed the first proceedings, when the case comes on again " may I be there to see.'

CHAPTER V.

"Every Englishman's house is his castle,"
"I scorn the foreign yoke," and glory in the
name of Briton, and all that. The natural
end, however, of all castles is to be burnt or
blown up. In England it is true you can
call the constable, and should any foreign
power attack you with grinding organ and
white mice, you may hope for succours from
without, from which cause "castles" in England are more long lived. In New Zealand,
however, it is different, as, to the present
day, the old system prevails, and castles continue to be disposed of in the natural way, as
has been seen lately at Taranaki.

I now purchased a piece of land and built
a "castle" for myself. I really can't tell to
the present day who I purchased the land
from, for there were about fifty different

claimants, every one of whom assured me
that the other forty-nine were "humbugs,"
and had no right whatever. The nature of
the different titles of the different claimants
were various. One man said his ancestors
had killed off the first owners; another declared his ancestors had driven off the second
party; another man, who seemed to be
listened to with more respect than ordinary,
declared that his ancestor had been the first
possessor of all, and had never been ousted,
and that this ancestor was a huge lizard that
lived in a cave on the land many ages ago,
and sure enough there was the cave to prove
it. Besides the principal claims there were
an immense number of secondary ones—a
sort of latent equities — which had lain
dormant until it was known the pakeha had
his eye on the land. Some of them seemed
to me at the time odd enough. One man
required payment because his ancestors, as
he affirmed, had exercised the right of catch-
ing rats on it, but which he (the claimant)
had never done, for the best of reasons, *i.e.*,
there were no rats to catch, except indeed
pakeha rats, which were plenty enough,
but this variety of rodent was not counted
as game. Another claimed because his

grandfather had been murdered on the
land, and—as I am a veracious pakeha—
another claimed payment because *his* grandfather had committed the murder ! Then
half the country claimed payments of various
value, from one fig of tobacco to a musket,
on account of a certain *wahi tapu,* or
ancient burying-ground, which was on the
land, and in which every one almost had had
relations or rather ancestors buried, as they
could clearly make out, in old times, though
no one had been deposited in it for about two
hundred years, and the bones of the others
had been (as they said) removed long ago to
a *torere* in the mountains. It seemed an
awkward circumstance that there was some
difference of opinion as to where this same
wahi tapu was situated, being, and lying, for
in case of my buying the land it was stipu-
lated that I should fence it round and make
no use of it, although I had paid for it. (I,
however, have put off fencing till the exact
boundaries have been made out ; and indeed
I don't think I shall ever be called on to do
so, the fencing proviso having been made, as I
now believe, to give a stronger look of reality
to the existence of the sacred spot, it having
been observed that I had some doubts on the

subject. No mention was ever made of it after the payments had been all made, and so I think I may venture to affirm that the existence of the said *wahi tapu* is of very doubtful authenticity, though it certainly cost me a round "lot of trade.") There was one old man who obstinately persisted in declaring that he, and he alone, was the sole and rightful owner of the land; he seemed also to have a "fixed idea" about certain barrels of gunpowder; but as he did not prove his claim to my satisfaction, and as he had no one to back him, I of course gave him nothing; he nevertheless demanded the gunpowder about once a month for five-and-twenty years, till at last he died of old age, and I am now a landed proprietor, clear of all claims and demands, and have an undeniable right to hold my estate as long as ever I am able.

It took about three months' negotiation before the purchase of the land could be made; and, indeed, I at one time gave up the idea, as I found it quite impossible to decide who to pay. If I paid one party, the others vowed I should never have possession, and to pay all seemed impossible; so at last I let all parties know that I had made up my mind not to have the land. This, however, turned out to be the first step I had made in the right direction ; for, thereupon, all the different claimants agreed amongst themselves to demand a certain quantity of goods, and divide them amongst themselves afterwards. I was glad of this, for I wished to buy the land, as I thought, in case I should ever take a trip to the "colonies," it would look well to be able to talk of "my estate in New Zealand." The day being now come on which I was to make the payment, and all parties present, I then and there handed over to the assembled mob the price of the land, consisting of a great lot of blankets, muskets, tomahawks, tobacco, spades, axes, &c., &c.; and received in return a very dirty piece of paper with all their marks on it, I having written the terms of transfer on it in English to my own perfect satisfaction. The cost per acre to me was, as near as can be, about five and a half times what the same quantity of land would have cost me at the same time in Tasmania ; but this was not of much importance, as the value of land in New Zealand then, and indeed now, being chiefly imaginary, one could just as easily suppose it to be of a very great value as a very small one; I therefore did not complain of the cost.

While I am on the subject of land and land titles, I may as well here mention that many years after the purchase of my land I received notice to appear before certain persons called " Land Commissioners," who were part and parcel of the new inventions which had come up soon after the arrival of the first governor, and which are still a trouble to the land. I was informed that I must appear and prove my title to the land I have mentioned, on pain of forfeiture of the same. Now I could not see what right any one could have to plague me in this way, and if I had had no one but the commissioners and two or three hundred men of their tribe to deal with, I should have put my pa in fighting order, and told them to "come on ;" for before this time I had had occasion to build a pa, (a little misunderstanding,) and being a re- gularly naturalised member of a strong tribe, could raise men to defend it at the shortest notice. But somehow these people had cunningly managed to mix up the name of Queen Victoria, God bless her ! (no disparagement to King Potatau) in the matter ; and I, though a pakeha Maori, am a loyal subject to her Majesty, and will stick up and fight for her as long as ever I can

G

muster a good imitation of courage or a leg to stand upon. This being the case, I made a very unwilling appearance at the court, and explained and defended my title to the land in an oration of four hours' and a half duration ; and which, though I was much out of practice, I flatter myself was a good specimen of English rhetoric, and which, for its own merits as well as for another reason which I was not aware of at the time, was listened to by the court with the greatest patience. When I had concluded, and having been asked " if I had any more to say ? " I saw the commissioner beginning to count my words, which had been all written I suppose in short hand ; and having ascertained how many thousand I had spoken, he handed me a bill, in which I was charged by the word, for every word I had spoken, at the rate of one farthing and one twentieth per word. Oh, Cicero ! Oh, Demosthenes ! Oh, Pitt, Fox, Burke, Sheridan ! Oh, Daniel O'Connell ! what would have become of you, if such a stopper had been clapt on your jawing tackle ? Fame would never have cracked her trumpet, and " Dan " would never have raised the *rint*. For my part I have never recovered the shock. I have since that time become taciturn, and have adopted a Spartan brevity when forced to speak, and I fear I shall never again have the full swing of my mother tongue. Besides this, I was charged ten shillings each for a little army of witnesses who I had brought by way of being on the sure side—five shillings a head for calling them into court, and five more for "examining" them; said examination consisting of one question each, after which they were told to "be off." I do believe had I brought up a whole tribe, as I had thoughts of doing, the commissioners would not have minded examining them all. They were, I am bound to say, very civil and polite; one of them told me I was "a damned, infernal, clever fellow, and he should like to see a good many more like me." I hope I am not getting tedious, but this business made such an impression on me, that I can't help being too prolix, perhaps, when describing it. I have, however, often since that time had my doubts whether the Queen (God bless her) got the money or knew half as much of the affair as they wanted to make out. I *don't* believe it. Our noble Queen would be clean above such a proceeding; and I mean to say its against Magna Charta, it is! "Justice shall *not be sold,*" saith Magna Charta ; and if it's not selling justice to make a loyal pakeha Maori pay for every word he speaks when defending his rights in a court of justice, I don't know what is.

Well, to make matters up, they after some time gave me a title for my land (as if I had not one before) ; but then, after some years, they made me give it back again, on purpose, as they said, that they might give me a better ! But since that time several more years have passed, and I have not got it ; so, as these things are now all the fashion, " I wish I may get it."

CHAPTER VI.

I NEVER yet could get the proper knack of
telling a story. Here I am now, a good forty
years ahead of where I ought to be, talking
of "title deeds" and "land commissioners,"
things belonging to the new and deplorable
state of affairs which began when this country
became "a British colony and possession,"
and also "one of the brightest jewels in the
British crown." I must go back.

Having purchased my "estate," I set up
housekeeping. My house was a good com-
modious *raupo* building; and as I had a
princely income of a few hundred a year "in
trade," I kept house in a very magnificent and
hospitable style. I kept always eight stout
paid Maori retainers, the pay being one fig of
tobacco per week, and their potatoes, which
was about as much more. Their duties were

not heavy; being chiefly to amuse themselves fishing, wrestling, shooting pigeons, or pig-hunting, with an occasional pull in the boat when I went on a water excursion. Besides these paid retainers, there was always about a dozen hangers on, who considered themselves a part of the establishment, and who, no doubt, managed to live at my expense; but as that expense was merely a few hundred weight of potatoes a week, and an odd pig now and then, it was not perceptible in the good old times. Indeed these hangers on, as I call them, were necessary; for now and then, in those brave old times, little experiments would be made by certain Maori gentlemen of freebooting propensities, and who were in great want of "British manufactures," to see what could be got by bullying "the pakeha," and to whom a good display of physical force was the only argument worth notice. These gentry generally came from a long distance, made a sudden appearance, and, thanks to my faithful re-tainers, who, as a matter of course, were all bound to fight for me, though I should have found it hard to get much *work* out of them, made as sudden a retreat, though on one or two occasions, when my standing army were accidentally absent, I had to do battle single handed. I think I have promised somewhere that I would perform a single combat for the amusement of the ladies, and so I may as well do it now as at any other time. I shall, therefore, recount a little affair I had with one of these gentry, as it is indeed quite necessary I should, if I am to give any true idea of "the good old times." I must, however, protest against the misdeeds of a few ruffians—human wolves—being charged against the whole of their countrymen. At the time I am speaking of, the only restraint on such people was the fear of retaliation, and the consequence was, that often a dare-devil savage would run a long career of murder, robbery, and outrage, before meeting with a check, simply from the terror he inspired, and the "luck" which often accompanies outrageous daring. At a time, however, and in a country like New Zealand, where every man was a fighting man or nothing, these desperadoes, sooner or later, came to grief, being at last invariably shot, or run through the body, by some sturdy freeholder, whose rights they had invaded. I had two friends staying with me, young men who had come to see me from the neighbouring colonies, and to take a summer tour in New Zealand; and it so happened

that no less than three times during my
absence from home, and when I had taken
almost all my people along with me, my castle
had been invaded by one of the most notorious
ruffians who had ever been an impersonation
of, or lived by, the law of force. This interesting specimen of the *genus homo* had, on the
last of these visits, demanded that my friends
should hand over to him one pair of blankets ;
but as the prospectus he produced, with
respect to payment, was not at all satisfactory,
my friends declined to enter into the speculation, the more particularly as the blankets
were mine. Our freebooting acquaintance
then, to explain his views more clearly,
knocked both my friends down ; threatened
to kill them both with his tomahawk ; then
rushed into the bed-room, dragged out all
the bed-clothes, and burnt them on the
kitchen fire.

This last affair was rather displeasing to me.
I held to the theory that every Englishman's
house was his castle, and was moreover rather
savage at my guests having been so roughly
handled. I in fact began to feel that though
I had up to this time managed to hold my
own pretty well, I was at last in danger of
falling under the imposition of " black mail,"

and losing my *status* as an independent potentate—a *rangatira* of the first water. I then and there declared loudly that it was well for the offender that I had not been at home, and that if ever he tried his tricks with *me* he would find out his mistake. These declarations of war, I perceived, were heard by my men in a sort of incredulous silence, (silence in New Zealand gives *dis*-sent,) and though the fellows were stout chaps, who would not mind a row with any ordinary mortal, I verily believe they would have all ran at the first appearance of this redoubted ruffian. Indeed his antecedents had been such as might have almost been their excuse. He had killed several men in fair fight, and had also—as was well known—committed two most diabolical murders, one of which was on his own wife, a fine young woman, whose brains he blew out at half a second's notice for no further provocation than this :—he was sitting in the verandah of his house, and told her to bring him a light for his pipe. She, being occupied in domestic affairs, said, "can't you fetch it yourself, I am going for water." She had the calibash in her hand and their infant child on her back. He snatched up his gun and instantly shot her dead on the spot; and I had heard him afterwards describing quite coolly the comical way in which her brains had been knocked out by the shot with which the gun was loaded. He also had, for some trifling provocation, lopped off the arm of his own brother or cousin, I forget which, and was, altogether, from his tremendous bodily strength and utter insensibility to danger, about as "ugly a customer" as one would care to meet.

I am now describing a regular Maori ruffian of the good old times, the natural growth of a state of society wherein might was to a very great extent right, and where bodily strength and courage were almost the sole qualities for which a man was respected or valued. He was a bullet-headed, scowling, bow-legged, broad-shouldered, herculean savage, and all these qualifications combined made him unquestionably "a great *rangatira*," and, as he had never been defeated, his *mana* was in full force.

A few weeks after the affair of the blankets, as I was sitting all alone reading a Sydney newspaper, which, being only a year old, was highly interesting, my friends and all my natives having gone on an expedition to haul a large fishing net, who should I see enter

the room and squat down on the floor, as if
taking permanent possession, but the amiable
and highly interesting individual I have taken
so much trouble to describe. He said
nothing, but his posture and countenance
spoke whole volumes of defiance and mur-
derous intent. He had heard of the threats
I had made against him, and there he was,
let me turn him out if I dare. That was his
meaning,—there was no mistaking it.

I have all my life been an admirer of the
suaviter in modo, though it is quite out of
place in New Zealand. If you tell a man—
a Maori I mean—in a gentle tone of voice and
with a quiet manner that if he continues a
given line of conduct you will begin to commence to knock him down, he simply disbe-
lieves you, and thereby forces you to do that
which, if you could have persuaded yourself
to have spoken very uncivilly at first, there
would have been no occasion for. I have
seen many proofs of this, and though I have
done my best for many years to improve the
understanding of my Maori friends in this
particular, I find still there are but very few
who can understand at all how it is possible
that the *suaviter in modo* can be combined
with the *fortiter in re*. They in fact can't

understand it for some reason perfectly inex-
plicable to me. It was, however, quite a
matter of indifference, I could perceive, how
I should open proceedings with my friend, as
he evidently meant mischief. "Habit is
second nature," so I instinctively took to the
suaviter. "Friend," said I, in a very mild
tone and with as amiable a smile as I could
get up, in spite of a certain clenching of the
teeth which somehow came on me at the
moment, "my advice to you is to be off." He
seemed to nestle himself firmer in his seat, and
made no answer but a scowl of defiance. "I am
thinking, friend, that this is my house," said I,
and springing upon him I placed my foot to his
shoulder, and gave a shove which would have
sent most people heels over-head. Not so,
however, with my friend. It shook him,
certainly, a little ; but in an instant, as quick
as lightning, and as it appeared with a single
motion, he bounded from the ground, flung
his mat away over his head, and struck a
furious blow at my head with his tomahawk.
I escaped instant death by a quickness equal
to or greater than his own. My eye was
quick, and so was my arm ; life was at stake.
I caught the tomahawk in full descent ; the
edge grazed my hand ; but my arm, stiffened

like a bar of iron, arrested the blow. He made one furious, but ineffectual, effort to tear the tomahawk from my grasp; and then we seized one another round the middle, and struggled like maniacs in the endeavour to dash each other against the boarded floor, I holding on for dear life to the tomahawk, and making desperate efforts to get it from him, but without a chance of success, as it was fastened to his wrist by a strong thong of leather. He was, as I soon found, somewhat stronger than me, and heavier; but I was as active as a cat, and as long winded as an emu, and very far from weak. At last he got a *wiri* round my leg; and had it not been for the table on which we both fell, and which, in smashing to pieces, broke our fall, I might have been disabled and in that case instantly tomahawked. We now rolled over and over on the floor like two mad bulldogs; he trying to bite, and I trying to stun him by dashing his bullet head against the floor. Up again! —still both holding on to the tomahawk. Another furious struggle, in the course of which both our heads, and half our bodies, were dashed through the two glass windows in the room, and every single article of furniture was reduced to atoms. Down again, rolling like mad, and dancing about amongst the rubbish—the wreck of the house. By this time we were both covered with blood from various wounds, received I don't know how. I had been all this time fighting under a great disadvantage, for my friend was trying to kill me, and I was only trying to disarm and tie him up—a much harder thing than to kill. My reason for going to this trouble was, that as there were no witnesses to the row, if I killed him, I might have had serious difficulties with his tribe. Up again; another terrific tussle for the tomahawk; down again with a crash; and so this life or death battle went on, down and up, up and down, for a full hour. At last I perceived that my friend was getting weaker, and felt that victory was only now a question of time. I, so far from being fatigued, was even stronger. Another desperate wrestling match. I lifted my friend high in my arms, and dashed him, panting, furious, foaming at the mouth, but *beaten*, against the ground. There he lies; the worshipper of force. His God has deserted him. But no, not yet. He has one more chance, and a fatal one it nearly proved to me. I began to unfasten the tomahawk from his wrist. An odd ex-

pression came over his countenance. He
spoke for the first time. "Enough, I am
beaten; let me rise." Now I had often
witnessed the manly and becoming manner
in which some Maoris can take defeat, when
they have been defeated in what they consider fair play. I had also ceased to fear
my friend, and so incautiously let go his
left arm. Like lightning he snatched at a
large carving fork, which, unperceived by
me, was lying on the floor amongst the
smashed furniture and *debris* of my household effects; his fingers touched the handle
and it rolled away out of his reach, and
my life was saved. He then struck me with
all his remaining force on the side of the
head, causing the blood to flow out of my
mouth. One more short struggle, and he was
conquered. But now I had at last got angry.
The drunkenness, the exhilaration of fight,
which comes on some constitutions, was fairly
on me. I had also a consciousness that now
I must kill my man, or, sooner or later, he
would kill me. I thought of the place I
would bury him; how I would stun him first
with the back of the tomahawk, to prevent
too much blood being seen; how I would
then carry him off (I could carry two such

men now, easy). I would *murder* him and cover him up. I unwound the tomahawk from his wrist: he was passive and helpless now. I wished he was stronger, and told him to get up and "die standing," as his countrymen say. I clutched the tomahawk for the *coup-de-grace*, (I can't help it, young ladies, the devil is in me,)—at this instant a thundering sound of feet is heard,—a whole tribe are coming! Now am I either lost or saved!—saved from doing that which I should afterwards repent, though constrained by necessity to do it. The rush of charging feet comes closer. In an instant comes dashing and smashing through doors and windows, in breathless haste and alarm, a whole tribe of friends. Small ceremony now with my antagonist. He was dragged by the heels, stamped on, kicked, and thrown half-dead, or nearly quite dead, into his canoe. All the time we had been fighting a little slave imp of a boy belonging to my antagonist had been loading the canoe with my goods and chattels, and had managed to make a very fair plunder of it. These were all now brought back by my friends, except one cloth jacket, which happened to be concealed under the *whariki*, and which I only mention because I remember

that the attempt to recover it some time afterwards cost one of my friends his life. The
savage scoundrel who had so nearly done for
me, broke two of his ribs, and so otherwise
injured him that he never recovered, and died
after lingering about a year. My friends
were going on a journey, and had called to
see me as they passed. They saw the slave
boy employed as I have stated, and knowing
to whom he belonged had rushed at once to
the rescue, little expecting to find me alive. I
may as well now dispose of this friend of
mine by giving his after history. He for a
long time after our fight went continually
armed with a double gun, and said he would
shoot me wherever he met me ; he however
had had enough of attacking me in my
"castle," and so did not call there any more.
I also went continually armed, and took care
also to have always some of my people at
hand. After this, this fellow committed two
more murders, and also killed in fair fight
with his own hand the first man in a native
battle, in which the numbers on each side
were about three hundred, and which I
witnessed. The man he killed was a remarkably fine young fellow, a great favourite of
mine. At last, having attacked and at-

tempted to murder another native, he was shot through the heart by the person he attempted to murder, and fell dead on the spot, and so there died "a great *rangatira*." His tribe quietly buried him and said no more about it, which showed their sense of right.   Had he been killed in what they considered an unjust manner, they would have revenged his death at any cost; but I have no doubt they themselves were glad to get rid of him, for he was a terror to all about him.   I have been in many a scrape both by sea and land, but I must confess that I never met a more able hand at an argument than this Maori *rangatira*.

I have not mentioned my friend's name with whom I had this discussion on the rights of Englishmen, because he has left a son, who is a great *rangatira*, and who might feel displeased if I was too particular, and I am not quite so able now to carry out a "face-to-face" policy as I was a great many years ago ; besides there is a sort of "honour amongst thieves" feeling between myself and my Maori friends on certain matters which we mutually understand are not for the ears of the "new people."

Now, ladies, I call that a fairish good fight,

considering no one is killed on either side. I promise to be good in future and to keep the peace, if people will let me ; and indeed, I may as well mention, that from that day to this I have never had occasion to explain again to a Maori how it is that "every Englishman's house is his castle."

"Fair play is a jewel ;" and I will here, as bound in honour to do, declare that I have met amongst the natives with men who would be a credit to any nation ; men on whom nature had plainly stamped the mark of "Noble," of the finest bodily form, quick and intelligent in mind, polite and brave, and capable of the most self-sacrificing acts for the good of others ; patient, forbearing, and affectionate in their families ; in a word, gentlemen. These men were the more remarkable, as they had grown up surrounded by a set of circumstances of the most unfavourable kind for the development of the qualities of which they were possessed ; and I have often looked on with admiration, when I have seen them protesting against, and endeavouring to restrain some of, the dreadful barbarities of their countrymen.

As for the Maori people in general, they are neither so good or so bad as their friends and enemies have painted them, and I suspect are pretty much like what almost any other people would have become, if subjected for ages to the same external circumstances. For ages they have struggled against necessity in all its shapes. This has given to them a remarkable greediness for gain in every visible and immediately tangible form. It has even left its mark on their language. Without the aid of iron the most trifling tool or utensil could only be purchased by an enormously disproportionate outlay of labour in its construction, and, in consequence, became precious to a degree scarcely conceivable by people of civilised and wealthy countries. This great value attached to personal property of all kinds, increased proportionately the tempta- tion to plunder; and where no law existed, or could exist, of sufficient force to repress the inclination, every man, as a natural con- sequence, became a soldier, if it were only for the defence of his own property and that of those who were banded with him—his tribe, or family. From this state of things regular warfare arose, as a matter of course; the military art was studied as a science, and brought to great perfection as applied to the arms used; and a marked military character was given to the people. The necessity of labour, the necessity of warfare, and a temperate climate, gave them strength of body, accompanied by a perseverance and energy of mind, perfectly astonishing. With rude and blunt stones they felled the giant kauri—toughest of pines ; and from it, in process of time, at an expense of labour, perseverance, and ingenuity, perfectly astounding to those who know what it really was—produced, carved, painted, and inlaid, a masterpiece of art, and an object of beauty,—the war canoe, capable of carrying a hundred men on a distant expedition, through the boisterous seas surrounding their island.

As a consequence of their warlike habits and character, they are self-possessed and confident in themselves and their own powers, and have much diplomatic finesse and casuistry at command. Their intelligence causes them theoretically to acknowledge the benefits of law, which they see established amongst us, but their hatred of restraint causes them practically to abhor and resist its full enforcement amongst themselves. Doubting our professions of friendship, fearing our ultimate designs, led astray by false friends, possessed of that " little learning,"

which is, in their case, most emphatically
" a dangerous thing," divided amongst themselves,—such are the people with whom we
are now in contact,—such the people to whom,
for our own safety and their preservation, we
must give new laws and institutions, new
habits of life, new ideas, sentiments and information,—whom we must either civilise or
by our mere contact exterminate. How is
this to be done ?* Let me see. I think I
shall answer this question when I am prime
minister.

---

* PRINTER'S DEVIL :—How is *this* to be done ?—*which ?*
what ?—how ?—*civilise* or *exterminate ?* PAKEHA MAORI :
—*Eaha mau !*

CHAPTER VII.

THE natives have been for fifty years or more
in a continual state of excitement on one
subject or another, which has had a markedly
bad effect on their character and physical
condition, as I shall by-and-by take occasion
to point out. When the first straggling ships
came here the smallest bit of iron was a prize
so inestimable that I might be thought to
exaggerate were I to tell the bare truth on
the subject. The excitement and speculation
caused by a ship being seen off the coast was
immense. Where would she anchor ? What
iron could be got from her ? Would it be
possible to seize her ? The oracle was consulted, preparations were made to follow her
along the coast, even through an enemy's

country, at all risks ; and when she disappeared she was not forgotten, and would continue long to be the subject of anxious expectation and speculation.

After this, regular trading began. The great madness then was for muskets and gunpowder. A furious competition was kept up. Should any tribe fail to procure a stock of these articles as soon as its neighbours, extermination was its probable doom. We may then imagine the excitement, the over-labour, the hardship, the starvation (occasioned by crops neglected whilst labouring to produce flax or other commodity demanded in payment)—I say imagine, but I have seen at least part of it.

After the demand for arms was supplied, came a perfect furor for iron tools, instruments of husbandry, clothing, and all kinds of pakeha manufactures. These things having been quite beyond their means while they were supplying themselves with arms, they were in the most extreme want of them, particularly iron tools. A few years ago the madness ran upon horses and cattle ; and now young New Zealand believes in nothing but money, and they are continually tormenting themselves with plans to acquire it in large sums at once, without the trouble of slow and saving industry, which, as applied to the accumulation of money, they neither approve of nor understand ; nor will they ever, as a people, take this mode till convinced that money, like everything else of value, can only be procured as a rule by giving full value for it, either in labour or the produce of labour.

Here I am, I find, again before my story. Right down to the present time talking of " young New Zealand," and within a hair's-breadth of settling " the Maori difficulty " without having been paid for it, which would have been a great oversight, and contrary to the customs of New Zealand. I must go back.

There were in the old times two great institutions, which reigned with iron rod in Maori land—the *Tapu* and the *Muru*. Pakehas who knew no better, called the *muru* simply "robbery," because the word *muru*, in its common signification, means to plunder. But I speak of the regular legalised and established system of plundering as penalty for offences, which in a rough way resembled our law by which a man is obliged to pay "damages." Great abuses had, however, crept into this system—so great, indeed, as

to render the retention of any sort of moveable property almost an impossibility, and
to in a great measure discourage the inclination to labour for its acquisition. These
great inconveniences were, however, met, or
in some degree softened, by an expedient of
a peculiarly Maori nature, which I shall
by-and-by explain. The offences for which
people were plundered were sometimes of a
nature which, to a *mere* pakeha, would seem
curious. A man's child fell in the fire and
was almost burnt to death. The father was
immediately plundered to an extent that
almost left him without the means of subsistence : fishing nets, canoes, pigs, provisions
—all went. His canoe upset, and he and all
his family narrowly escaped drowning—some
were, perhaps, drowned. He was immediately
robbed, and well pummelled with a club into
the bargain, if he was not good at the science
of self-defence—the club part of the ceremony
being always fairly administered one against
one, and after fair warning given to defend
himself. He might be clearing some land for
potatoes, burning off the fern, and the fire
spreads farther than he intended, and gets
into a *wahi tapu* or burial-ground. No
matter whether any one has been buried in it

or no for the last hundred years, he is
tremendously robbed. In fact for ten
thousand different causes a man might be
robbed ; and I can really imagine a case
in which a man for scratching his own head
might be legally robbed. Now as the en-
forcers of this law were also the parties who
received the damages, as well as the judges of
the amount, which in many cases (such as that
of the burnt child) would be everything they
could by any means lay hands on, it is easy
to perceive that under such a system personal
property was an evanescent sort of thing
altogether. These executions or distraint
were never resisted. Indeed in many cases,
as I shall explain by-and-by, it would have
been felt as a slight, and even an insult, *no*
to be robbed ; the sacking of a man's establishment being often taken as a high compliment, especially if his head was broken into
the bargain ; and to resist the execution
would not only have been looked upon as
mean and disgraceful in the highest degree,
but it would have debarred the contemptible
individual from the privilege of robbing his
neighbours, which was the compensating expedient I have alluded to. All this may
seem a waste of words to my pakeha Maori

readers, to whom these things have become such matters of course as to be no longer remarkable ; but I have remembered that there are so many new people in the country who don't understand the beauty of being knocked down and robbed, that I shall say a few more words on the subject.

The tract of country inhabited by a single tribe might be say from forty to a hundred miles square, and the different villages of the different sections of the tribe would be scattered over this area at different distances from each other. We will by way of illustrating the working of the *muru* system take the case of the burnt child. Soon after the accident it would be heard of in the neighbouring villages ; the family of the mother are probably the inhabitants of one of them ; they have, according to the law of *muru*, the first and greatest right to clean out the afflicted father—a child being considered to belong to the family of the mother more than to that of the father—in fact it is their child, who the father has the rearing of. The child was moreover a promising lump of a boy, the makings of a future warrior, and consequently very valuable to the whole tribe in general, but to the mother's family in particular.

"A pretty thing to let him get spoiled." Then
he is a boy of good family, a *rangatira* by
birth, and it would never do to let the thing
pass without making a noise about it. That
would be an insult to the dignity of the families of both father and mother. Decidedly,
besides being robbed, the father must be
assaulted with the spear. True, he is a
famous spearman, and for his own credit
must "hurt" some one or another if attacked.
But this is of no consequence ; a flesh wound
more or less deep is to be counted on ; and
then think of the plunder ! It is against the
law of *muru* that any one should be killed,
and first blood ends the duel. Then the
natural affection of all the child's relations
is great. They are all in a great state of
excitement, and trying to remember how
many canoes, and pigs, and other valuable
articles, the father has got : for this must be
a clean sweep. A strong party is now mustered, headed probably by the brother of the
mother of the child. He is a stout chap, and
carries a long tough spear. A messenger is
sent to the father, to say that the *taua muru*
is coming, and may be expected to-morrow, or
the next day. He asks, " Is it a great *taua* ?"
" Yes ; it is a very great *taua* indeed."

The victim smiles, he feels highly complimented, he *is* then a man of consequence. His child is also of great consideration ; he is thought worthy of a. large force being sent to rob him ! Now he sets all in motion to prepare a huge feast for the friendly robbers his relations. He may as well be liberal, for his provisions are sure to go, whether or no. Pigs are killed and baked whole, potatoes are piled up in great heaps, all is made ready, he looks out his best spear, and keeps it always ready in his hand. At last the *taua* appears on a hill half a mile off ; then the whole fighting men of the section of the tribe of which he is an important member, collect at his back, all armed with spear and club, to shew that they could resist, if they would— a thing, however, not to be thought of under the circumstances. On comes the *taua*. The mother begins to cry in proper form ; the tribe shout the call of welcome to the approaching robbers ; and then with a grand rush, all armed, and looking as if they intended to exterminate all before them, the *kai muru* appear on the scene. They dance the war dance, which the villagers answer with another. Then the chief's brother-in-law advances, spear in hand, with the most

alarming gestures. " Stand up !—stand up !
I will kill you this day," is his cry. The
defendant is not slow to answer the challenge.
A most exciting, and what to a new pakeha
would appear a most desperately dangerous,
fencing bout with spears, instantly commences.
The attack and defence are in the highest degree scientific ; the spear shafts keep up a
continuous rattle ; the thrust, and parry, and
stroke with the spear shaft follow each other
with almost incredible rapidity, and are too
rapid to be followed by an unpractised eye.
At last the brother-in-law is slightly touched ;
blood also drops from our chief's thigh. The
fight instantly ceases ; leaning on their spears,
probably a little badinage takes place between them, and then the brother-in-law
roars out " *murua! murua! murua!* " Then
the new arrivals commence a regular sack,
and the two principals sit down quietly with
a few others for a friendly chat, in which
the child's name is never mentioned, or the
enquiry as to whether he is dead or alive even
made. The case I have just described would,
however, be one of more than ordinary importance ; slighter " accidents and offences "
would be atoned for by a milder form of
operation. But the general effect was to keep

personal property circulating from hand to
hand pretty briskly, or indeed to convert it
into public property ; for no man could say
who would be the owner of his canoe, or
blanket, in a month's time. Indeed, in that
space of time, I once saw a nice coat, which
a native had got from the captain of a trading
schooner, and which was an article much
coveted in those days, pass through the
hands, and over the backs, of six different
owners, and return, considerably the worse
for wear, to the original purchaser ; and all
these transfers had been made by legal process
of *muru*. I have been often myself paid the
compliment of being robbed for little accidents occurring in my family, and have several
times also, from a feeling of politeness, robbed
my Maori friends, though I can't say I was a
great gainer by these transactions. I think the
greatest haul I ever made was about half a
bag of shot, which I thought a famous joke,
seeing that I had sold it the day before to the
owner for full value. A month after this I
was disturbed early in the morning, by a
voice shouting " Get up !—get' up ! I will
kill you this day. You have roasted my
grandfather. Get up !—*stand* up ! " I, of
course, guessed that I had committed some

heinous though involuntary offence, and the
"stand up" hinted the immediate probable
consequences ; so out I turned, spear in hand,
and who should I see, armed with a bayonet
on the end of a long pole, but my friend the
unwhile owner of the bag of shot. He came
at me with pretended fury, made some smart
bangs and thrusts, which I parried, and then
explained to me that I had "cooked his grandfather ;" and that if I did not come down
handsome in the way of damages, deeply as
he might regret the necessity, his own credit,
and the law of *muru*, compelled him either to
sack my house or die in the attempt. I was
glad enough to prevent either event, by paying
him two whole bags of shot, two blankets,
divers fish hooks, and certain figs of tobacco,
which he demanded. I found that I had
really and truly committed a most horrid
crime. I had on a journey made my fire at
the foot of a tree, in the top of which the
bones of my friend's grandfather had once
been deposited, but from which they had been
removed ten years before ; the tree caught fire
and had burnt down : and I, therefore, by
a convenient sort of figure of speech, had
"roasted his grandfather," and had to pay
the penalty accordingly.

It did not require much financial ability on my part, after a few experiences of this nature, to perceive that I had better avail myself of my privileges as a pakeha, and have nothing further to do with the law of *muru*—a determination I have kept to strictly. If ever I have unwittingly injured any of my neighbours, I have always made what I considered just compensation, and resisted the *muru* altogether; and I will say this for my friends, that when any of them have done an accidental piece of mischief, they have, in most cases without being asked, offered to pay for it.

The above slight sketch of the penal law of New Zealand I present and dedicate to the Law Lords of England, as it might, perhaps, afford some hints for a reform in our own. The only remark I shall have to add is, that if a man killed another, "malice prepence aforethought," the act, in nineteen cases out of twenty, would be either a very meritorious one, or of no consequence whatever; in either of which cases the penal code had, of course, nothing to do in the matter. If, however, a man killed another by *accident*, in the majority of cases the consequences would be most serious; and not only the involuntary homicide, but every one connected with him, would be plundered of everything they possessed worth taking. This, however, to an English lawyer, may require some explanation, which is as follows :—If a man thought fit to kill his own slave, it was nobody's affair but his own ; the law had nothing to do with it. If he killed a man of another tribe, he had nothing to do but declare it was in revenge or retaliation for some aggression, either recent or traditional, by the other tribe, of which examples were never scarce. In this case the action became at once highly meritorious, and his whole tribe would support and defend him to the last extremity. If he, however, killed a man by accident, the slain man would be, as a matter of course, in most instances, one of his ordinary companions—*i.e.*, one of his own tribe. The accidental · discharge of a gun often caused death in this way. Then, indeed, the law of *muru* had full swing, and the wholesale plunder of the criminal and family was the penalty. Murder, as the natives understood it, that is to say, the malicious destruction of a man of *the same tribe*, did not happen as frequently as might be expected ; and when it did, went in most cases unpunished ; the murderer, in general, man-

aging to escape to some other section of the
tribe where he had relations, who, as he fled
to them for protection, were bound to give it,
and always ready to do so; or otherwise he
would stand his ground and defy all comers,
by means of the strength of his own family
or section, who all would defend him and
protect him as a mere matter of course; and
as the law of *utu* or *lex talionis* was the only
one which applied in this case, and as, unlike
the law of *muru*, nothing was to be got by
enforcing it but hard blows, murder in most
cases went unpunished.

CHAPTER VIII.

THE law of *muru* is now but little used, and
only on a small scale. The degenerate men
of the present day in general content themselves with asking "payment," and after some
cavilling as to the amount, it is generally
given ; but if refused, the case is brought
before a native magistrate, and the pleadings
on both sides are often such as would astound
our most famous barristers, and the decisions
of a nature to throw those famous ones by
Sancho Panza and Walter the Doubter for
ever into the shade.

I think the reason that the *muru* is so
much less practised than formerly is the fact
that the natives are now far better supplied
with the necessaries and comforts of life than
they were many years ago, especially iron tools

and utensils, and in consequence the temptation to plunder is proportionately decreased. Money would still be a temptation ; but it is so easily concealed, and in general they have so little of it, that other means are adopted for its acquisition. When I first saw the natives, the chance of getting an axe or a spade by the short-hand process of *muru*, or—at a still more remote period — a few wooden implements, or a canoe, was so great that the lucky possessor was continually watched by many eager and observant eyes, in hopes to pick a hole in his coat, by which the *muru* might be legally brought to bear upon him. I say legally, for the natives always tried to have a sufficient excuse ; and I absolutely declare, odd as it may seem, that actual, un-authorised, and inexcusable robbery or theft was less frequent than in any country I ever have been in, though the temptation to steal was a thousandfold greater. The natives of the present day are, however, improving in this respect, and, amongst other arts of civilisation, are beginning to have very pretty notions of housebreaking, and have even tried highway robbery, though in a bungling way. The fact is they are just now between two tides. The old institutions which, barbarous and rude as they were, were respected and in some degree useful, are wearing out, and have lost all beneficial effect, and at the same time the laws and usages of civilisation have not acquired any sufficient force. This state of things is very unfavourable to the *morale* of Young New Zealand; but it is likely to change for the better, for it is a maxim of mine that "laws, if not *made*, will *grow*."

I must now take some little notice of the other great institution, the *tapu*. The limits of these flying sketches of the good old times will not allow of more than a partial notice of the all-pervading *tapu*. Earth, air, fire, water, goods and chattels, growing crops, men, women, and children,—everything absolutely was subject to its influence, and a more perplexing puzzle to new pakehas who were continually from ignorance infringing some of its rules, could not be well imagined. The natives, however, made considerable allowance for this ignorance, as well they might, seeing that they themselves, though from infancy to old age enveloped in a cloud of *tapu*, would sometimes fall into similar scrapes.

The original object of the ordinary *tapu* seems to have been the preservation of property. Of this nature in a great degree was the ordinary personal *tapu*.   This form of the *tapu* was permanent, and consisted in a certain sacred character which attached to the person of a chief and never left him.   It was his birthright, a part in fact of himself, of which he could not be divested, and which was well understood and recognised at all times as a matter of course.   The fighting men and petty chiefs, and every one indeed who could by any means claim the title of *rangatira*— which in the sense I now use it means gentleman—were all in some degree more or less possessed of this mysterious quality.   It extended or was communicated to all their moveable property, especially to their clothes, weapons, ornaments, and tools, and to every thing in fact which they touched. This prevented their chattels from being stolen or mislaid, or spoiled by children, or used or handled in any way by others.   And as in the old times, as I have before stated, every kind of property of this kind was precious in consequence of the great labour and time necessarily, for want of iron tools, expended in the manufacture, this form of the *tapu* was of great real service.   An infringement of it subjected the offender to various dreadful imaginary punishments, of which deadly sickness was one, as well as to the operation of the law of *muru* already mentioned. If the transgression was involuntary, the chief, or a priest, or *tohunga*, could, by a certain mystical ceremony, prevent or remit the doleful and mysterious part of the punishment if he chose, but the civil action, or the robbery by law of *muru*, would most likely have to take its course, though possibly in a mitigated form, according to the circumstances.

I have stated that the worst part of the punishment of an offence against this form of the *tapu* was imaginary, but in truth, though imaginary it was not the less a severe punishment. "Conscience makes cowards of us all," and there was scarcely a man in a thousand, *if* one, who had sufficient resolution to dare the shadowy terrors of the *tapu*. I actually have seen an instance where the offender, though an involuntary one, was killed stone dead in six hours, by what I considered the effects of his own terrified imagination, but what all the natives at the time believed to be the work of the terrible avenger of the *tapu*. The case I may as well describe, as it was a strong one, and shows how, when falsehoods are once believed, they will meet with apparent proof from accidental circumstances. A chief of very high rank, standing, and *mana*, was on a war expedition ; with him were about five hundred men. His own personal *tapu* was increased two-fold, as was that of all the warriors who were with him, by the *war tapu.* The *taua* being on a very dangerous expedition, they were over and above the ordinary personal *tapu* made sacred in the highest degree, and were obliged to observe strictly several mysterious and sacred customs, some of which I may have to explain by-and-by. They were, in fact, as irreverent pakehas used to say, " tabooed an inch thick," and as for the head chief, he was perfectly unapproachable. The expedition halted to dine. The portion of food set apart for the chief, in a neat *paro* or shallow basket of green flax leaves, was, of course, enough for two or three men, and consequently the greater part remained unconsumed. The party having dined, moved on, and soon after a party of slaves and others, who had been some mile or two in the rear, came up carrying ammunition and baggage. One of the slaves, a stout hungry fellow, seeing the chief's unfinished dinner, eat it up before asking any questions, and had hardly finished when he

was informed by a horror-stricken individual
—another slave who had remained behind
when the *taua* had moved on—of the fatal
act he had committed. I knew the unfortunate delinquent well. He was remarkable
for courage, and had signalized himself in the
wars of the tribe. (The able-bodied slaves
are always expected to fight in the quarrels
of their masters, to do which they are
nothing loth.) No sooner did he hear the
fatal news than he was seized by the most
extraordinary convulsions and cramps in the
stomach, which never ceased till he died,
about sun-down the same day. He was a
strong man, in the prime of life, and if any
pakeha free-thinker should have said he was
not killed by the *tapu* of the chief, which had
been communicated to the food by contact, he
would have been listened to with feelings of
contempt for his ignorance and inability to
understand plain and direct evidence.

It will be seen at once that this form of the
tapu was a great preserver of property. The
most valuable articles might, in ordinary circumstances, be left to its protection, in the
absence of the owners, for any length of time.
It also prevented borrowing and lending in
a very great degree; and though much

laughed at and grumbled at by unthinking pakehas, who would be always trying to get the natives to give it up, without offering them anything equally effective in its place, or indeed knowing its real object or uses, it held its ground in full force for many years, and, in a certain but not so very observable a form, exists still. This form of the *tapu*, though latent in young folks of *rangatira* rank, was not supposed to develope itself fully till they had arrived at mature age, and set up house on their own account. The lads and boys " knocked about " amongst the slaves and lower orders, carried fuel or provisions on their backs, and did all those duties which this personal *tapu* prevented the elders from doing, and which restraint was sometimes very troublesome and inconvenient. A man of any standing could not carry provisions of any kind on his back, or if he did they were rendered *tapu*, and in consequence useless to any one but himself. If he went into the shed used as a kitchen, (a thing however he would never think of doing except on some great emergency,) all the pots, ovens, food, &c., would be at once rendered useless, —none of the cooks or inferior people could make use of them or partake of anything

which had been cooked in them. He might
certainly light a little fire in his own house,
not for cooking, as that never by any chance
could be done in his house, but for warmth ;
but that, or any other fire, if he should have
blown upon it with his breath in lighting it,
became at once *tapu*, and could be used for
no common or culinary purpose. Even to
light a pipe at it would subject any inferior
person, or in many instances an equal, to a
terrible attack of the *tapu morbus*, besides
being a slight or affront to the dignity of the
person himself. I have seen two or three
young men fairly wearing themselves out on
a wet day and with bad apparatus trying to
make fire to cook with, by rubbing two sticks
together, when on a journey, and at the same
time there was a roaring fire close at hand at
which several *rangatira* and myself were
warming ourselves, but it was *tapu*, sacred
fire—one of the *rangatira* had made it from
his own tinder box, and blown upon it in
lighting it, and as there was not another
tinder box amongst us, fast we must, though
hungry as sharks, till common culinary fire
could be obtained. A native whose personal
tapu was perhaps of the strongest, might,
when at the house of a pakeha, ask for a

drink of water ; the pakeha, being green, would hand him some water in a glass, or in those days, more probably in a tea-cup ; the native would drink the water, and then gravely and quietly break the cup to pieces, or otherwise he would appropriate it by causing it to vanish under his mat. The new pakeha would immediately fly into a passion, to the great astonishment of the native, who considered, as a matter of course, that the cup or glass was, in the estimation of the pakeha, a very worthless article, or he would not have given it into his hand and allowed him to put it to his head, the part most strongly infected by the *tapu*. Both parties would be surprised and displeased ; the native wondering what could have put the pakeha into such a taking, and the pakeha " wondering at the rascal's impudence, and what he meant by it ?" The proper line of conduct for the pakeha in the above case made and provided, supposing him to be of a hospitable and obliging disposition, would be to lay hold of some vessel containing about two gallons of water, (to allow for waste,) hold it up before the native's face, the native would then stoop down and put his hand bent into the shape of a funnel or conductor for the water to his

mouth ; then, from the height of a foot or
so, the pakeha would send a cataract of water
into the said funnel, and continue the shower
till the native gave a slight upward nod of
the head, which meant "enough"—by which
time, from the awkwardness of the pakeha,
the two gallons of water would be about expended, half, at least, on the top of the
native's head, who would not, however,
appear to notice the circumstance, and would
appreciate the civility of his pakeha friend.
I have often drank in this way in the old
times ; asking for a drink of water at a native
village, a native would gravely approach with
a calabash, and hold it up before me ready
to pour forth its contents ; I, of course,
cocked my hand and lip in the most knowing
manner. If I had laid hold of the calabash
and drank in the ordinary way as practised
by pakehas, I would have at once fallen in
the estimation of all by-standers, and been set
down as a *tutua*, a nobody, who had no *tapu*
or *mana* about him ; a mere scrub of a pakeha,
who any one might eat or drink after without
the slightest danger of being poisoned. These
things are all changed now, and though I
have often in the good old times been tabooed
in the most diabolical and dignified manner,

there are only a few old men left now who, by little unmistakable signs, I perceive consider it would be very uncivil to act in any way which would suppose my *tapu* to have disappeared before the influx of new-fangled pakeha notions. Indeed I feel myself sometimes as if I was somehow insensibly partially civilised. What it will all end in, I don't know.

This same personal *tapu* would even hold its own in some cases against the *muru*, though not in a sufficiently general manner to seriously affect the operation of that well-enforced law. Its inconveniences were, on the other hand, many, and the expedients resorted to to avoid them were sometimes comical enough. I was once going on an excursion with a number of natives ; we had two canoes, and one of them started a little before the other. I was with the canoe which had been left behind, and just as we were setting off it was discovered that amongst twenty stout fellows my companions there was no one who had a back !—as they expressed it—and consequently no one to carry our provisions into the canoe : all the lads, women, and slaves had gone off in the other canoe,—all those who had backs,—and

so there we were left, a very disconsolate lot of
rangatira, who could not carry their own provisions into the canoe, and who at the same
time could not go without them. The provisions consisted of several heavy baskets of
potatoes, some dried sharks, and a large pig
baked whole. What was to be done? We
were all brought to a full stop, though in a
great hurry to go on. We were beginning to
think we must give up the expedition altogether, and were very much disappointed
accordingly when a clever fellow, who, had
he been bred a lawyer, would have made
nothing of driving a mail coach through an
act of parliament, set us all to rights in a
moment. " I'll tell you what we must do,"
said he, " we will not carry (*pikau*) the provisions, we will *hiki* them." (*Hiki* is the
word in Maori which describes the act of
carrying an infant in the arms.) This was a
great discovery! A huge handsome fellow
seized on the baked pig and dandled it, or
hiki'd it, in his arms like an infant; another
laid hold of a shark, others took baskets of
potatoes, and carrying them in this way deposited them in the canoe. And so, having
thus evaded the law, we started on our
expedition.

I remember another amusing instance in which the inconvenience arising from the *tapu* was evaded. I must, however, notice that these instances were only evasions of the *tapu* of the ordinary kind,—what I have called the personal *tapu*,—not the more dangerous and dreadful kind connected with the mystic doings of the *tohunga*, or that other form of *tapu* connected with the handling of the dead. Indeed, my companions in the instance I have mentioned, though all *rangatira*, were young men on whom the personal *tapu* had not arrived at the fullest perfection ; it seemed, indeed, sometimes to sit very lightly on them, and I doubt very much if the play upon the words *hiki* and *pikau* would have reconciled any of the elders of the tribe to carrying a roasted pig in their arms, or if they did do so, I feel quite certain that no amount of argument would have persuaded the younger men to eat it ; as for slaves or women, to *look* at it would almost be dangerous to them.

The other instance of dodging the law was as follows. I was the first pakeha who had ever arrived at a certain populous inland village. The whole of the inhabitants were in a great state of commotion and curiosity, for many of them had never seen a pakeha before.

As I advanced, the whole juvenile population ran before me at a safe distance of about a hundred yards, eyeing me, as I perceived, with great terror and distrust. At last I suddenly made a charge at them, rolling my eyes and showing my teeth, and to see the small savages tumbling over one another and running for their lives was something curious, and though my "demonstration" did not continue more than twenty yards, I am sure some of the little villains ran a mile before looking behind to see whether the ferocious monster called a pakeha was gaining on them. They did run! I arrived at the centre of the village and was conducted to a large house or shed, which had been constructed as a place of reception for visitors, and as a general lounging place for all the inhabitants. It was a *whare noa*, a house to which, from its general and temporary uses, the *tapu* was not supposed to attach, I mean of course, the ordinary personal *tapu* or *tapu rangatira*. Any person, however, *infected* with any of the more serious or extraordinary forms of the *tapu* entering it, would at once render it uninhabitable. I took my seat. The house was full, and nearly the whole of the rest of the population were blocking up the open front of the large shed, all striving to see the pakeha, and passing to the rear from man to man every word he happened to speak. I could hear them say to the people behind, "The pakeha has stood up!" "Now he has sat down again!" "He has said, how do you all do?" "He has said, this is a nice place of yours!" etc., etc. Now there happened to be at a distance an old gentleman engaged in clearing the weeds from a *kumera* or sweet potato field, and as the kumera in the old times was the crop on which the natives depended chiefly for support, like all valuable things it was *tapu*, and the parties who entered the field to remove the weeds were *tapu*, *pro tem.*, also. Now one of the effects of this temporary extra *tapu* was that the parties could not enter any regular dwelling house, or indeed any house used by others. Now the breach of this rule would not be dangerous in a personal sense, but the effect would be that the crop of sweet potatoes would fail. The industrious individual I have alluded to, hearing the cry of "A pakeha! a pakeha!" from many voices, and having never had an opportunity to examine that variety of the species, or *genus homo,* flung down his wooden *kaheru* or weed exterminator and

rushed towards the town house before mentioned. What could he do ? The *tapu* forbid
his entrance and the front was so completely
blocked up by his admiring neighbours that
he could not get sight of the wonderful guest.
In these desperate circumstances a bright
thought struck him. He would, by a bold
and ingenious device, give the *tapu* the slip.
He ran to the back of the house, made with
some difficulty a hole in the padded *raupo*
wall, and squeezed his head through it. The
elastic wall of *raupo* closed again around his
neck ; the *tapu* was fairly beaten ! No one
could say he was *in* the house. He was certainly more out than in, and there, seemingly
hanging from or stuck against the wall, remained for hours, with open mouth and
wondering eyes, this brazen head, till at last
the shades of night obstructing its vision, a
rustling noise in the wall of flags and reeds
announced the departure of my bodyless
admirer.

Some of the forms of the *tapu* were not to
be played with, and were of a most virulent
kind. Of this kind was the *tapu* of those
who handled the dead, or conveyed the body
to its last resting-place. This *tapu* was, in
fact, the uncleanness of the old Jewish law,

and lasted about the same time, and was removed in almost the same way. It was a most serious affair. The person who came under this form of the *tapu* was cut off from all contact, and almost all communication, with the human race. He could not enter any house, or come in contact with any person or thing, without utterly bedeviling them. He could not even touch food with his hands, which had become so frightfully *tapu* or unclean, as to be quite useless. Food would be placed for him on the ground, and he would then sit or kneel down, and, with his hands carefully held behind his back, would gnaw it in the best way he could. In some cases he would be fed by another person, who, with outstretched arm, would manage to do it without touching the *tapu*'d individual; but this feeder was subjected to many and severe restrictions, not much less onerous than those to which the other was subject. In almost every populous native village there was a person who, probably for the sake of immunity from labour, or from being good for nothing else, took up the undertaking business as a regular profession, and, in consequence, was never for a moment, for years together, clear of the horrid inconveniences of the *tapu*, as well as its dangers. One of these people might be easily recognised, after a little experience, even by a pakeha. Old, withered, haggard, clothed in the most miserable rags, daubed all over from head to foot with red paint, (the native funereal colour,) made of stinking shark oil and red ochre mixed, keeping always at a distance, silent and solitary, often half insane, he might be seen sitting motionless all day at a distance, forty or fifty yards from the common path or thoroughfare of the village. There, under the " lee " of a bush, or tuft of flax, gazing silently, and with " lack-lustre eye," on the busy doings of the Maori world, of which he was hardly to be called a member. Twice a-day some food would be thrown on the ground before him, to gnaw as best he might, without the use of hands ; and at night, tightening his greasy rags around him, he would crawl into some miserable lair of leaves and rubbish, there, cold, half starved, miserable, and dirty, to pass, in fitful ghost - haunted slumbers, a wretched night, as prelude to another wretched day. It requires, they say, all ‧ sorts of people to make a world ; and I have often thought, in observing one of these miserable objects, that his, or her's, was the

very lowest ebb to which a human being's
prospects in life could be brought by adverse
fate. When I met, or rather saw, a female
practitioner, I fairly ran for it; and so, believing my readers to be equally tender-
hearted, I shall not venture on any more
description, but merely say that the man
undertaker, such as I have described him,
would be taken for Apollo if seen in one
of these hag's company.

What will my kind reader say when I tell
him that I myself once got *tapu*'d with this
same horrible, horrible, most horrible, style of
tapu? I hold it to be a fact that there is not
one man in New Zealand but myself who has
a clear understanding of what the word "ex-
communication" means, and I did not understand what it meant till I got *tapu*'d. I was
returning with about sixty men from a
journey along the west coast. I was a short
distance in advance of the party, when I
came to where the side of a hill had fallen
down on to the beach and exposed a number
of human bones. There was a large skull
rolling about in the water. I took up this
skull without consideration, carried it to the
side of the hill, scraped a hole, and covered it
up. Just as I had finished covering it up, up

came my friends, and I saw at once, by the astonishment and dismay depicted on their countenances, that I had committed some most unfortunate act. They soon let me know that the hill had been a burying-place of their tribe, and jumped at once to the conclusion that the skull was the skull of one of their most famous chiefs, whose name they told me, informing me also that I was no longer fit company for human beings, and begging me to fall to the rear and keep my distance. They told me all this from a very respectful distance, and if I made a step towards them, they all ran as if I had been infected by the plague. This was an awkward state of things, but as it could not be helped, I voted myself *tapu*, and kept clear of my friends till night. At night when they camped, I was obliged to take my solitary abode at a distance under shelter of a rock. When the evening meal was cooked, they brought me a fair allowance, and set it down at a respectful distance from where I sat, fully expecting, I suppose, that I should bob at it as Maori *kai tangi atua* or undertakers are wont to do. I had, however, no idea of any such proceeding; and pulling out my knife proceeded to operate in the usual

manner. I was checked by an exclamation of
horror and surprise from the whole band
—" Oh, what are you about, you are not
going to touch food with your *hands?*"
" Indeed, but I am," said I, and stretched
out my hand. Here another scream—" You
must not do that, it's the worst of all things ;
one of us will feed you ; it's wrong, wrong,
very wrong !" " Oh, bother," said I, and
fell too at once. I declare, positively, I had
no sooner done so than I felt sorry. The
expression of horror, contempt, and pity,
observable in their faces, convinced me that
I had not only offended and hurt their feelings, but that I had lowered myself greatly in
their estimation. Certainly I was a pakeha,
and pakehas will do most unaccountable
things, and may be, in ordinary cases,
excused ; but this, I saw at once, was an act
which, to my friends, seemed the *ne plus ultra*
of abomination. I now can well understand
that I must have, sitting there eating my
potatoes, appeared to them a ghoul, a vampire
—worse than even one of their own dreadful
atua, who, at the command of a witch, or to
avenge some breach of the *tapu*, enters into a
man's body and slowly eats away his vitals.
I can see it now, and understand what a

frightful object I must have appeared. My friends broke up their camp at once, not feeling sure, after what I had done, but I might walk in amongst them, in the night, when they were asleep, and bedevil them all. They marched all night, and in the morning came to my house, where they spread consternation and dismay amongst my household by telling them in what a condition I was coming home. The whole of my establishment at this time being natives, they ran at once; and when I got home next evening, hungry and vexed, there was not a soul to be seen. The house and kitchen were shut up, fires out, and, as I fancied, everything looked dreary and uncomfortable. If only a dog had come and wagged his tail in welcome, it would have been something; but even my dog was gone. Certainly there was an old tom cat, but I hate cats, there is no sincerity in them, and so I had kicked this old tom on principle whenever he came in my way, and now, when he saw me, he ran for his life into the bush. The instinct of a hungry man sent me into the kitchen; there was nothing eatable to be seen but a raw leg of pork, and the fire was out. I now began to suspect that this attempt of mine to look down the *tapu* would

fail, and that I should remain excommuni-
cated for some frightfully indefinite period.
I began to think of Robinson Crusoe, and to
wonder if I could hold out as well as he did.
Then I looked hard at the leg of pork. The
idea that I must cook for myself, brought
home to me the fact more forcibly than anything else how I had " fallen from my high
estate "—cooking being the very last thing a
rangatira can turn his hand to. But why
should I have anything more to do with
cooking ?—was I not cast off and repudiated
by the human race ? (A horrible misanthropy
was fast taking hold of me.) Why should I
not tear my leg of pork raw, like a wolf?
" I will run a muck ! "—suddenly said I. " I
wonder how many I can kill before they
'bag' me ? I will kill, kill, kill!—but—
I must have some supper."

I soon made a fire, and after a little rum-
maging found the *matériél* for a good meal.
My cooking was not so bad either, I thought ;
but certainly hunger is not hard to please in
this respect, and I had eaten nothing since
the diabolical meal of the preceding evening,
and had travelled more than twenty miles. I
washed my hands six or seven times, scrub-
bing away and muttering with an intonation

that would have been a fortune to a tragic actor. " Out damned spot ;" and so, after having washed and dried my hands, looked at them, returned, and washed again, again washed, and so on, several times, I sat down and demolished two days' allowance. After which, reclining before the fire with my pipe, and a blanket over my shoulders, a more kindly feeling towards my fellow men stole gradually upon me. " I wonder," said I to myself, " how long this devilish *tapu* will last ! I wonder if there is to be any end at all to it ! I won't run a muck for a week, at all events, till I see what may turn up. Confounded plague though to have to cook !" Having resolved as above, not to take any one's life for a week, I felt more patient. Four days passed somehow or another, and on the morning of the fifth, to my extreme delight, I saw a small canoe, pulled by one man, landing on the beach before the house. He fastened his canoe and advanced towards the kitchen, which was detached from the house, and which, in the late deplorable state of affairs, had become my regular residence. I sat in the doorway, and soon perceived that my visitor was a famous *tohunga*, or priest, and who also had the reputation of being a witch of no ordinary dimensions. He was an old, grave, stolid-looking savage, with one eye, the other had been knocked out long ago in a fight before he turned parson. On he came, with a slow, measured step, slightly gesticulating with one hand, and holding in the other a very small basket, not more than nine or ten inches long. He came on, mumbling and grumbling a perfectly unintelligible *karakia* or incantation. I guessed at once he was coming to disenchant me, and prepared my mind to submit to any conditions or ceremonial he should think fit to impose. My old friend came gravely up, and putting his hand into the little basket pulled out a baked *kumera*, saying, "*He kai mau.*" I of course accepted the offered food, took a bite, and as I ate he mumbled his incantation over me. I remember I felt a curious sensation at the time, like what I fancied a man must feel who had just sold himself, body and bones, to the devil. For a moment I asked myself the question whether I was not actually being then and there handed over to the powers of darkness. The thought startled me. There was I, an unworthy but believing member of the Church of England as by Parliament es-tablished, "knuckling down" abjectly to the

ministration of a ferocious old cannibal, wizard,
sorcerer, high priest,—as it appeared very
probable,—to Satan himself. "Blacken his
remaining eye ! knock him over and run the
country !" whispered quite plainly in my ear
my guardian angel, or else a little impul-
sive sprite who often made suggestions to
me in those days.   For a couple of seconds
the sorcerer's eye was in desperate danger :
but just in those moments the ceremony,
or at least this most objectionable part of it,
came to an end. He stood back and said,
"Have you been in the house ?" Fortu-
nately I had presence of mind enough to
forget that I had, and said, "No." "Throw
out all those pots and kettles." I saw it was
no use to resist—so out they went. "Fling
out those dishes" was the next command.
"The dishes !—they will break." "I am
going to break them all." Capital fun this.
--out go the dishes ; "and may the ——."
I fear I was about to say something bad.
"Fling out those knives, and those things
with sharp points"—(the old villain did not
know what to call the forks !) --"and those
shells with handles to them"—(spoons!)—"out
with everything." The last sweeping order is
obeyed, and the kitchen is fairly empty. The

worst is over now at last, thank goodness,
said I to myself. " Strip off all your clothes."
" What ?—strip naked !—you desperate old
thief—mind your eye." Human patience
could bear no more. Out I jumped. I did
" strip." Off came my jacket. " How would
you prefer being killed, old ruffian ?—can you
do anything in this way ?" (Here a pugilistic
demonstration.) " Strip !—he doesn't mean to
give me five dozen, does he ? " said I, rather
bewildered, and looking sharp to see if he had
anything like an instrument of flaggellation in
his possession. " Come on !—what are you
waiting for," said I. In those days, when
labouring under what Dickens calls the " description of temporary insanity which arises
from a sense of injury," I always involuntarily
fell back upon my mother tongue, which in
this case was perhaps fortunate, as my necro-
mantic old friend did not understand the full
force of my eloquence. He could not, however, mistake my warlike and rebellious atti-
tude, and could see clearly I was going into
one of those most unaccountable rages that
pakehas were liable to fly into, without any
imaginable cause. " Boy," said he, gravely
and quietly, and without seeming to notice
my very noticeable declaration of war and

independence, "don't act foolishly; don't
go mad. No one will ever come near you
while you have those clothes. You will be
miserable here by yourself. And what is the
use of being angry?—what will *anger* do for
you?" The perfect coolness of my old friend,
the complete disregard he paid to my ex-
plosion of wrath, as well as his reasoning,
began to make me feel a little disconcerted.
He evidently had come with the purpose and
intention to get me out of a very awkward
scrape. I began also to feel that, looking at
the affair from his point of view, I was just
possibly not making a very respectable figure ;
and then, if I understood him rightly, there
would be no *flogging*. "Well," said I, at
last, "Fate compels ; to fate, and not old
Hurlo-thrumbo there, I yield—so here goes."
Let me not dwell upon the humiliating concession to the powers of *tapu*. Suffice it to
say, I disrobed, and received permission to
enter my own house in search of other gar-
ments. When I came out again, my old
friend was sitting down with a stone in his
hand, battering the last pot to pieces, and
looking as if he was performing a very
meritorious action. He carried away all the
smashed kitchen utensils and my clothes in

L

baskets, and deposited them in a thicket at a considerable distance from the house. (I stole the knives, forks, and spoons back again some time after, as he had not broken them.) He then bid me good bye; and the same evening all my household came flocking back : but years passed before any one but myself would go into the kitchen, and I had to build another. And for several years also I could observe, by the respectable distance kept by young natives and servants, and the nervous manner with which they avoided my pipe in particular, that they considered I had not been as completely purified from the *tapu tango atua* as I might have been. I now am aware, that in consideration of my being a pakeha, and also perhaps, lest driven to desperation, I should run away entirely, which would have been looked upon as a great misfortune to the tribe, I was let off very easy, and might therefore be supposed to retain some tinge of the dreadful infection.

Besides these descriptions of *tapu*, there were many other. There was the *war tapu*, which in itself included fifty different " sacred customs," one of which was this—that often when the fighting men left the pa or camp, they being themselves made *tapu*, or sacred, as in this particular case the word means, all those who remained behind, old men, women, slaves, and all noncombatants were obliged strictly to fast while the warriors were fighting ; and, indeed, from the time they left the camp till their return, even to smoke a pipe would be a breach of this rule. These war customs, as well as other forms of the *tapu*, are evidently derived from a very ancient religion, and did not take their rise in this country. I shall, probably, some of these days, treat of them at more length, and endeavour to trace them to their source.

Sacrifices were often made to the war demon, and I know of one instance in which, when a tribe were surrounded by an overwhelming force of their enemies, and had nothing but extermination—immediate and unrelenting—before them, the war chief cut out the heart of his own son as an offering for victory, and then he and his tribe, with the fury of despair and the courage of fanatics, rushed upon the foe, defeated them with terrific slaughter, and the war demon had much praise, and many men were eaten.

The warriors, when on a dangerous expedition, also observed strictly the custom to which allusion is made. 1st Samuel, xxi., 4-5.

CHAPTER IX.

THEN came the *tapu tohunga,* or priest's *tapu,*
a quite different kind or form of *tapu* from
those which I have spoken of. These *tohunga*
presided over all those ceremonies and
customs which had something approaching
to a religious character. They also pretended to the power—by means of certain
familiar spirits—to foretel future events, and
even in some cases to control them. The
belief in the power of these *tohunga* to foretel
events was very strong, and the incredulous
pakeha who laughed at them was thought a
person quite incapable of understanding plain
evidence. I must allow that some of their
predictions were of a most daring nature, and
happening to turn out perfectly successful,
there may be some excuse for an ignorant
people believing in them. Most of these
predictions were, however, given—like the

oracles of old—in terms which would admit a double meaning and secure the character of the soothsayer no matter how the event turned out. It is also remarkable that these *tohunga* did not pretend to divine future events by any knowledge or power existing in themselves; they pretended to be for the time inspired by the familiar spirit, and passive in his hands. This spirit "entered into" them, and, on being questioned, gave a response in a sort of half whistling half articulate voice, supposed to be the proper language of spirits; and I have known a *tohunga* who, having made a false prediction, laid the blame on the "tricksey spirit," who he said had purposely spoken false for certain good and sufficient spiritual reasons, which he then explained. Amongst the fading customs and beliefs of the good old times the *tohunga* still holds his ground, and the oracle is as often consulted, though not so openly, as it was a hundred years ago, and is as firmly believed in; and this by natives who are professed Christians; and the enquiries are often on subjects of the most vital importance to the welfare of the colony. A certain *tohunga* has even quite lately, to my certain knowledge, been paid a large sum of money to do a miracle ! I saw the money paid, and I saw the miracle. And the miracle was a good enough sort of miracle, as miracles go in these times, The natives know we laugh at their belief in these things. They would much rather we were angry, for then they would defy us; but as we simply laugh at their credulity, they do all they can to conceal it from us; but nevertheless the chiefs, on all matters of importance, continue to consult the Maori oracle.

I shall give two instances of predictions which came under my own observation, and which will show how much the same priest-craft has been in all times.

A man—a petty chief—had a serious quarrel with his relations, left his tribe, and went to a distant part of the country, saying that he cast them off and would never return. After a time the relations became both un-easy at his absence and sorry for the disagree-ment. The presence of the head of the family was also of consequence to them. They therefore enquired of the oracle if he would return. At night the *tohunga* invoked the familiar spirit, he became inspired, and in a sort of hollow whistle came the words of fate :—"He will return ; but yet not return."

This response was given several times, and then the spirit departed, leaving the priest or *tohunga* to the guidance of his own unaided wits. No one could understand the meaning of the response. The priest himself said he could make nothing of it. The spirit of course knew his own meaning; but all agreed that, whatever that meaning was, it would turn out true. Now the conclusion of this story is rather extraordinary. Some time after this several of the chief's relations went to offer reconciliation and to endeavour to persuade him to return home. Six months afterwards they returned, bringing him along with them *a corpse:* they had found him dying, and carried his body home. Now all knew the meaning of the words of the oracle, " He will return, but yet not return."

Another instance, which I witnessed myself, was as follows :—A captain of a large ship had run away with a Maori girl ; or a Maori girl had run away with a ship captain ; I should not like to swear which is the proper form of expression ; and the relations, as in such cases happens in most countries, thought it incumbent on them to get into a great taking, and make as much noise as possible about the matter. Off they set to the *tohunga,*

I happened to be at his place at the time, and saw and heard all I am about to recount. The relations of the girl did not merely confine themselves to asking questions, they demanded active assistance. The ship had gone to sea loaded for a long voyage. The fugitives had fairly escaped; and what the relations wanted was that the *atua*, or familiar spirit of the *tohunga*, should bring the ship back into port, so that they might have an opportunity to recover the lost ornament of the family. I heard the whole. The priest hummed and hawed. "He did not know, could not say. We should hear what the 'boy' would say. He would do as he liked. Could not compel him;" and so forth. At night all assembled in the house where the priest usually performed. All was expectation. I saw I was *de trop* in the opinion of our soothsayer; in fact, I had got the name of an infidel, (which I have since taken care to get rid of,) and the spirit was unwilling to enter the company of unbelievers. My friend the priest hinted to me politely that a nice bed had been made for me in the next house. I thanked him in the most approved Maori fashion, but said I was "very comfortable where I was;" and, suiting the action to the word, rolled my cloak about me, and lay down on the rushes with which the floor was covered. About midnight I heard the spirit saluting the guests, and they saluting him ; and I also noticed they hailed him as " relation," and then gravely preferred the request that he would " drive back the ship which had stolen his cousin." The response, after a short time, came in the hollow mysterious whistling voice,—" The ship's nose I will batter out on the great sea." This answer was repeated several times, and then the spirit departed, and would not be recalled. The rest of the night was spent in conjecturing what could be the meaning of these words. All agreed that there must be more in them than met the ear ; but no one could say it was a clear concession of the request made. As for the priest, he said he could not understand it, and that " the spirit was a great rogue "—a *koroke hangareka*. He, however, kept throwing out hints now and then that something more than common was meant, and talked generally in the " we shall see " style. Now here comes the end of the affair. About ten days after this in comes the ship. She had been " battered " with a vengeance. She had been met by a terrible gale when a couple of hundred miles off the land, and had sprung a leak in the bow. The bow in Maori is called the "nose" *(ihu)*. The vessel had been in great danger, and had been actually forced to run for the nearest port, which happened to be the one she had left. Now, after such a coincidence as this, I can hardly blame the ignorant natives for believing in the oracle, for I actually caught myself quoting, " Can the devil speak truth ?" Indeed I have in the good old times known several pakehas who "thought there was something in it," and two who formally and believingly consulted the oracle, and paid a high *douceur* to the priest.

I shall give one more instance of the response of the Maori oracle. A certain northern tribe, noted for their valour, but not very numerous, sent the whole of their best men on a war expedition to the south. This happened about forty years ago. Before the *taua* started the oracle was consulted, and the answer to the question, " Shall this expedition be successful ?" came. " A desolate country ! —a desolate country !—a desolate country !" This the eager warriors accepted as a most favourable response. They said the enemy's country would be desolated. It, however, so turned out that they were all exterminated to a man, and the miserable remnant of their tribe, weakened and rendered helpless by their loss, became a prey to their more immediate neighbours, lost their lands, and have ceased from that day to be heard of as an independent tribe. So, in fact, it was the country of the eager enquirers which was laid "desolate." Every one praised the oracle, and its character was held higher than ever.

CHAPTER X.

THE PRIEST EVOKES A SPIRIT—THE CONSEQUENCES—A
MAORI TRAGEDY—THE "TOHUNGA" AGAIN.

THESE priests or *tohunga* would, and do to
this hour, undertake to call up the spirit of
any dead person, if paid for the same. I have
seen many of these exhibitions, but one instance will suffice as an example.

A young chief, who had been very popular
and greatly respected in his tribe, had been
killed in battle ; and, at the request of several
of his nearest friends, the *tohunga* had promised on a certain night to call up his spirit
to speak to them, and answer certain questions
they wished to put. The priest was to come to
the village of the relations, and the interview
was to take place in a large house common to
all the population. This young man had been
a great friend of mine ; and so, the day before
the event, I was sent to by his relations, and
told that an opportunity offered of conversing
with my friend once more. I was not much

inclined to bear a part in such outrageous mummery, but curiosity caused me to go. Now it is necessary to remark that this young chief was a man in advance of his times and people in many respects. He was the first of his tribe who could read and write ; and, amongst other unusual things for a native to do, he kept a register of deaths and births, and a journal of any remarkable events which happened in the tribe. Now this book was lost. No one could find it, although his friends had searched unceasingly for it, as it contained many matters of interest, and also they wished to preserve it for his sake. I also wished to get it, and had often inquired if it had been found, but had always been answered in the negative. The appointed time came, and at night we all met the priest in the large house I have mentioned. Fires were lit, which gave an uncertain flickering light. The priest retired to the darkest corner. All was expectation, and the silence was only broken by the sobbing of the sister, and other female relations of the dead man. They seemed to be, and indeed were, in an agony of excite-ment, agitation, and grief. This state of things continued for a long time, and I began to feel in a way surprising to myself, as if

there was something real in the matter. The
heart-breaking sobs of the women, and the
grave and solemn silence of the men, convinced me, that to them at least, this was a
serious matter. I saw the brother of the
dead man now and then wiping the tears in
silence from his eyes. I wished I had not
come, for I felt that any unintentional
symptom of incredulity on my part would
shock and hurt the feelings of my friends
extremely ; and yet, whilst feeling thus, I
felt myself more and more near to believing
in the deception about to be practised. The
real grief, and also the general undoubting
faith, in all around me, had this effect. We
were all seated on the rush-strewn floor ;
about thirty persons. The door was shut ;
the fire had burnt down, leaving nothing but
glowing charcoal. The room was oppressively
hot. The light was little better than darkness ; and the part of the room in which the
tohunga sat was now in perfect darkness.
Suddenly, without the slightest warning, a
voice came out of the darkness. " Salutation !—salutation to you all !—salutation !—
salutation to you my tribe !—family I salute
you !—friends I salute you !—friend, my pakeha
friend, I salute you." The high-handed daring

imposture was successful; our feelings were taken by storm. A cry expressive of affection and despair, such as was not good to hear, came from the sister of the dead chief, a fine, stately, and really handsome woman of about five-and-twenty. She was rushing, with both arms extended, into the dark, in the direction from whence the voice came. She was instantly seized round the waist and restrained by her brother by main force, till moaning and fainting she lay still on the ground. At the same instant another female voice was heard from a young girl who was held by the wrists by two young men, her brothers. "Is it you?—is it you?—*truly* is it you?—*aue!* *aue!* they hold me, they restrain me; wonder not that I have not followed you; they restrain me, they watch me, but I go to you. The sun shall not rise, the sun shall not rise, *aue! aue!*" Here she fell insensible on the rush floor, and with the sister was carried out. The remaining women were all weeping and exclaiming, but were silenced by the men who were themselves nearly as much excited, though not so clamorous. I, however, did notice two old men, who sat close to me, were not in the slightest degree moved in any way, though they did not seem at all incredulous, but quite the contrary. The Spirit spoke again. "Speak to me, the tribe!—speak to me, the family!—speak to me the pakeha!" The "pakeha," however, was not at the moment inclined for conversation. The deep distress of the two women, the evident belief of all around him of the presence of the spirit, the "darkness visible," the novelty of the scene, gave rise to a state of feeling not favourable to the conversational powers. Besides, I felt reluctant to give too much apparent credence to an imposture, which at the very same time, by some strange impulse, I felt half ready to give way to. At last the brother spoke— "How is it with you?—is it well with you in *that* country?" The answer came—(the voice all through, it is to be remembered, was not the voice of the *tohunga* but a strange melancholy sound, like the sound of the wind blowing into a hollow vessel,)—"It is well with me—my place is a good place." The brother spoke again—"Have you seen ——, and ——, and —— ?" (I forget the names mentioned.) "Yes, they are all with me." A woman's voice now from another part of the room anxiously cried out—"Have you seen my sister?" "Yes, I have seen her." "Tell her my love is great towards

her and never will cease." "Yes, I will tell."
Here the woman burst into tears and the
pakeha felt a strange swelling of the chest,
which he could in no way account for.
The Spirit spoke again. "Give my large
tame pig to the priest, (the pakeha was disen-
chanted at once,) and my double-gun." Here
the brother interrupted—"Your gun is a
manatunga, I shall keep it." He is also dis-
enchanted, thought I, but I was mistaken.
He believed, but wished to keep the gun his
brother had carried so long. An idea now
struck me that I could expose the imposture
without showing palpable disbelief. "We
cannot find your book," said I, "where have
you concealed it?" The answer instantly
came, "I concealed it between the *tahuhu* of my
house and the thatch, straight over you as you
go in at the door." Here the brother rushed
out,—all was silence till his return. In five
minutes he came back *with the book in his
hand*. I was beaten, but made another effort.
—"What have you written in that book?" said
I. "A great many things." "Tell me some
of them." "Which of them?" "Any of
them." "You are seeking for some information, what do you want to know? I
will tell you." Then suddenly—"Farewell,

M

O tribe! farewell, my family, I go!" Here
a general and impressive cry of "farewell"
arose from every one in the house. "Farewell," again cried the spirit, *from deep beneath the ground!* "Farewell," again from
high in air! "Farewell," once more came
moaning through the distant darkness of the
night. "Farewell!" I was for a moment
stunned. The deception was perfect. There
was a dead silence—at last. "A ventrilo-
quist," said I!—" or—or—*perhaps* the devil."

I was fagged and confused. It was past
midnight; the company broke up, and I
went to a house where a bed had been prepared for me. I wished to be quiet and
alone; but it was fated there should be little
quiet that night. I was just falling asleep,
after having thought for some time on the
extraordinary scenes I had witnessed, when I
heard the report of a musket at some little
distance, followed by the shouting of men and
the screams of women. Out I rushed. I
had a presentiment of some horrible catas-
trophe. Men were running by, hastily
armed. I could get no information, so went
with the stream. There was a bright flame
beginning to spring up at a short distance,
and every one appeared going in that direc-

tion : I was soon there. A house had been set on fire to make a light. Before another house, close at hand, a dense circle of human beings was formed. I pushed my way through, and then saw, by the bright light of the flaming house, a scene which is still fresh before me : there, in the verandah of the house, was an old grey-bearded man ; he knelt upon one knee, and on the other he supported the dead body of the young girl who had said she would follow the spirit to spirit land. The delicate-looking body from the waist upwards was bare and bloody ; the old man's right arm was under the neck, the lower part of his long grey beard was dabbled with blood, his left hand was twisting his matted hair ; he did not weep, he *howled*, and the sound was that of a heathen despair, knowing no hope. The young girl had secretly procured a loaded musket, tied a loop for her foot to the trigger, placed the muzzle to her tender breast, and blown herself to shatters. And the old man was her father, and a *tohunga*. A calm low voice now spoke close beside me, " She has followed her *rangatira*," it said. I looked round, and saw the famous *tohunga* of the night.

Now, young ladies, I have promised not to

frighten your little wits out with raw-head-and-bloody-bones stories, a sort of thing I detest, but which has been too much the fashion with folks who write of matters Maori. I have vowed not to draw a drop of blood except in a characteristic manner. But this story is tragedy, or I don't know what tragedy is, and the more tragic because, in every particular, literally true, and so if you cannot find some pity for the poor Maori girl who "followed her lord to spirit land," I shall make it my business not to fall in love with any of you any more for I won't say how long.

CHAPTER XI.

A STORY-TELLER, like a poet or a pugilist,
must be *born*, and not *made*, and I begin to
fancy I have not been born under a story-
telling planet, for by no effort that I can make
can I hold on to the thread of my story, and
I am conscious the whole affair is fast becoming one great parenthesis. If I could only get
clear of this *tapu* I would "try back." I believe I ought to be just now completing the
purchase of my estate. I am sure I have
been keeping house a long time before it
is built, which is I believe clear against the
rules, so I must get rid of this talk about
the *tapu* the best way I can, after which I
will start fair and try not to get before my
story.

Besides these different forms of the *tapu*
which I have mentioned, there were endless

others, but the temporary local *tapus* were the most tormenting to a pakeha, as well they might, seeing that even a native could not steer clear of them always. A place not *tapu* yesterday might be most horribly *tapu* to-day, and the consequences of trespassing thereon proportionately troublesome. Thus, sailing along a coast or a river bank, the most inviting landing-place would be almost to a certainty the freehold property of the Taniwha, a terrific sea monster, who would to a certainty, if his landed property was trespassed on, upset the canoe of the trespassers and devour them all the very next time they put to sea. The place was *tapu*, and let the weather be as bad as it might, it was better to keep to sea at all risks than to land there. Even pakeha, though in some cases invulnerable, could not escape the fangs of the terrible Taniwha. "Was not little Jackey-*poto*, the sailor, drowned by the Taniwha? He *would* go on shore, in spite of every warning, to get some water to mix with his *waipiro*, and was not his canoe found next day floating about with his paddle and two empty case bottles in it?—a sure sign that the Taniwha had lifted him out bodily. And was not the body of the said Jackey found some days after with the Taniwha's mark on it,—one eye taken out ? "

These Taniwha would, however, sometimes attach themselves to a chief or warrior, and in the shape of a huge sea monster, a bird, or a fish, gambol round his canoe, and by their motions give presage of good or evil fortune.

When the Ngati Kuri sailed on their last and fated expedition to the south, a huge Taniwha, attached to the famous warrior, Tiki Whenua, accompanied the expedition, playing about continually amongst the canoes, often coming close to the canoe of Tiki Whenua, so that the warrior could reach to pat him approvingly with his paddle, at which he seemed much pleased ; and when they came in sight of the island of Tuhua, this Taniwha chief called up the legions of the deep ! The sea was blackened by an army of monsters, who, with uncouth and awful floundering and wallowing, performed before the chief and his companions a hideous *tu ngarahu*, and then disappeared. The Ngati Kuri, elated, and accepting this as a presage of victory, landed on Tuhua, stormed the pa, and massacred its defenders. But they had mistaken the meaning of the monster review of the Taniwha. It was a leave-

taking of his favourite warrior, for the Ngati
Kuri were fated to die to a man on the next
land they trod. A hundred and fifty men were
they—the pick and prime of their tribe. All
rangatira, all warriors of name, few in numbers, but desperately resolute, they thought it
little to defeat the thousands of the south, and
take the women and children as a prey! Having feasted and rejoiced at Tuhua, they sail for
Motiti. This world was too small for them.
They were impatient for battle. They thought
to make the name of Kuri strike against the
skies; but in the morning the sea is covered
with war canoes. The thousands of the south
are upon them! Ngati Awa, with many an
allied band, mad for revenge, come on. Fight
now, oh Ngati Kuri!—not for *victory*, no, nor
for *life*. Think only now of *utu!*—for your
time is come. That which you have dealt to
many, you shall now receive. Fight!—fight!
Your tribe shall be exterminated, but you
must leave a name! Now came the tug of
war on "bare Motiti." From early morning till
the sun had well declined, that ruthless battle
raged. Twice their own number had the
Ngati Kuri slain; and then Tiki Whenua,
still living, saw around him his dead and
dying tribe. A handful of bleeding warriors

still resisted—a last and momentary struggle. He thought of the *utu* ; it was great. He thought of the ruined remnant of the tribe at home, and then he remembered—horrid thought—that ere next day's setting sun, he and all the warriors of his tribe would be baked and eaten. (Tiki, my friend, thou art in trouble.)   A cannon was close at hand—a nine pound carronade. They had brought it in the canoes.   Hurriedly he filled it half full of powder, seized a long fire brand, placed his breast to the cannon's mouth, fired with his own hand.   Tiki Whenua, Good night !

Now I wonder if Brutus had had such a thing as a nine-pounder about him at Phillippi, whether he would have thought of using it in this way.   I really don't think he would.   I have never looked upon Brutus as anything of an original genius, but Tiki Whenua most certainly was.   I don't think there is another instance of a man blowing himself from a gun —of course there are many examples of people blowing others from cannon, but that is quite a different thing—any blockhead can do that. But the *exit* of Tiki Whenua has a smack of originality about it which I like, and so I have mentioned it here.

But all this is digression on digression ;

however, I suppose the reader is getting used
to it, and I cannot help it; besides I wanted
to show them how poor Tiki "took arms
against a sea of troubles," and for the want of
a "bare bodkin" made shift with a carronade.
I shall never cease to lament those nice lads
who met with that little accident (poor fellows!) on Motiti. A fine, strapping, stalwart
set of fellows, who believed in force. We
don't see many such men now-a-days; the
present generation of Maori are a stunted,
tobacco-smoking, grog-drinking, psalm-sing-
ing, special-pleading, shilling-hunting set of
wretches; not above one in a dozen of them
would know how to cut up a man *secundem
artem*. 'Pshaw! I am ashamed of them.

I am getting tired of this *tapu*, so will give
only one or two more instances of the local
temporary *tapu*. In the autumn, when the
great crop of *kumera* was gathered, all the
paths leading to the village and cultivated
lands were made *tapu*, and any one coming
along them would have notice of this by
finding a rope stretched across the road about
breast-high; when he saw this, his business
must be very urgent indeed or he would go
back, and it would have been taken as a very
serious affront indeed, even in a near relation,

supposing his ordinary residence was not in
the village, to disregard the hint given by the
rope,—that for the present there was "no
thoroughfare." Now, the reason of this
blockade of the roads was this. The report of
an unusually fine crop of *kumera* had often
cost its cultivators and the whole tribe their
lives. The news would spread about that
Ngati so-and-so, living at so-and-so, had
housed so many thousands of baskets of
kumera. Exaggeration would multiply the
truth by ten, the fertile land would be
coveted, and very probably its owners, or
rather its *holders*, would have to fight both
for it and their lives before the year was out.
For this reason strangers were not welcome
at the Maori harvest home. The *kumera*
were dug hurriedly by the whole strength of
the working hands, thrown in scattered heaps,
and concealed from any casual observation by
strangers by being covered over with the
leaves of the plants, and when all were dug
then all hands set to work, at night, to fill the
baskets and carry off the crop to the store-
house or *rua*, and every effort was made to get
all stored and out of sight before daylight, lest
any one should be able to form any idea of
the extent of the crop. When the digging of

one field was completed another would be done in the same manner, and so on till the whole crop was housed in this stealthy manner. I have been at several of these midnight labours, and have admired the immense amount of work one family would do in a single night, working as it were for life and death. In consequence of this mode of proceeding, even the families inhabiting the same village did not know what sort of a crop their neighbours had, and if a question was asked, (to do which was thought impertinent and very improper,) the invariable answer was, "Nothing at all; barely got back the seed; hardly that; we shall be starved; we shall have to eat fern root this year," &c. The last time I observed this custom was about twenty-seven years ago, and even then it was nearly discontinued and no longer general.

Talking of by-gone habits and customs of the natives, I remember I have mentioned two cases of suicide. I shall, therefore, now take occasion to state that no more marked alteration in the habits of the natives has taken place than in the great decrease of cases of suicide. In the first years of my residence in the country, it was of almost daily occurrence. When a man died, it was almost a matter of course that his wife, or wives, hung themselves. When the wife died, the man very commonly shot himself. I have known young men, often on the most trifling affront or vexation, shoot themselves; and 1 was acquainted with a man who, having been for two days plagued with the toothache, cut his throat with a very blunt razor, without a handle, as a radical cure, which it certainly was. I do not believe that one case of suicide occurs now, for twenty when I first came into the country. Indeed, the last case I have heard of in a populous district, occurred several years ago. It was rather a remarkable one. A native owed another a few shillings; the creditor kept continually asking for it; but the debtor, somehow or other, never could raise the cash. At last, being out of patience, and not knowing anything of the Insolvent Court, he loaded his gun, went to the creditor's house, and called him out. Out came the creditor and his wife. The debtor then placed the gun to his own breast, and saying, "Here is your payment," pulled the trigger with his foot, and fell dead before them. I think the reason suicide has become so comparatively unfrequent is, that the minds of the natives are now filled and agitated by a flood of new ideas, new wants and ambitions, which they know not formerly, and which prevents them, from one single loss or disappointment, feeling as if there was nothing more to live for.

CHAPTER XII.

There was a kind of variation on the *tapu*,
called *tapa*, of this nature. For instance, if a
chief said, "That axe is my head," the axe
became his to all intents and purposes, except,
indeed, the owner of the axe was able to
break his "head," in which case, I have reason
to believe, the *tapa* would fall to the ground.
It was, however, in a certain degree necessary
to have some legal reason, or excuse, for
making the *tapa*; but to give some idea of
what constituted the circumstances under
which a man could fairly *tapa* anything, I
must needs quote a case in point.

When the Ngapuhi attacked the tribe of
Ngati Wakawe, at Rotorua, the Ngati Wakawe retired to the island of Mokoia in the
lake of Rotorua, which they fortified, thinking
that, as the Ngapuhi canoes could not come
nearer than Kaituna on the east coast, about

thirty miles distant, that they in their island
position would be safe. But in this they
were fatally deceived, for the Ngapuhi
dragged a whole fleet of war canoes over
land. When, however, the advanced division
of the Ngapuhi arrived at Rotorua, and en-
camped on the shore of the lake, Ngati
Wakawe were not aware that the canoes of
the enemy were coming, so every morning
they manned their large canoes, and leaving
the island fort, would come dashing along the
shore deriding the Ngapuhi, and crying,
"*Ma wai koe e kawe mai ki Rangitiki?*"—
"Who shall bring you, or how shall you
arrive, at Rangitiki?" Rangitiki was the
name of one of their hill forts. The canoes were
fine large ornamented *totara* canoes, very
valuable, capable of carrying from fifty to
seventy men each, and much coveted by the
Ngapuhi. The Ngapuhi of course considered
all these canoes as their own already, but the
different chiefs and leaders, anxious to secure
one or more of these fine canoes for themselves and people, and not knowing who
might be the first to lay hands on them in
the confusion of the storming of Mokoia,
which would take place when their own canoes
arrived, each *tapa'd* one or more for himself,

or—as the native expression is—*to* himself.
Up jumped Pomare, and standing on the lake
shore in front of the encampment of the division of which he was leader, he shouts—
pointing at the same time to a particular
canoe at the time carrying about sixty men—
"That canoe is my back-bone." Then Tareha,
in bulk like a sea elephant, and sinking to
the ancles in the shore of the lake, with a
hoarse croaking voice roars out, "That canoe!
my skull shall be the bailer to bail it out." This
was a horribly strong *tapu*. Then the soft
voice of the famous Hongi Ika, surnamed
"The eater of men," of *Hongi kai tangata*,
was heard, "Those two canoes are my two
thighs." And so the whole flotilla was appropriated by the different chiefs. Now it
followed from this that in the storming and
plunder of Mokoia, when a warrior clap't his
hand on a canoe and shouted, "This canoe is
mine," the seizure would not stand good if it
was one of the canoes which were *tapu-tapu*,
for it would be a frightful insult to Pomare to
claim to be the owner of his "back-bone," or
to Tareha to go on board a canoe which had
been made sacred by the bare supposition that
his "skull" should be a vessel to bail it with.
Of course the first man laying his hand on

any other canoe and claiming it secured it for himself and tribe, always provided that the number of men there present representing his tribe or *hapu* were sufficient to back his claim and render it dangerous to dispossess him. I have seen men shamefully robbed, for want of sufficient support, of their honest lawful gains, after all the trouble and risk they had gone to in killing the owners of their plunder. But dishonest people are to be found almost everywhere, and I will say this, that my friends the Maoris seldom act against law, and always try to be able to say what they do is "correct"—(*tika*).

This *tapu* is a bore, even to write about, and I fear the reader is beginning to think it a bore to read about. It began long before the time of Moses, and I think that steam navigation will be the death of it; but lest it should kill my reader I will have done with it for the present, and "try back," for I have left my story behind completely.

CHAPTER XIII.

WHEN I purchased my land the payment
was made on the ground, and immediately
divided and subdivided amongst the different
sellers. Some of them, who, according to their
own representations formerly made to me,
were the sole and only owners of the land,
received for their share about the value of one
shilling, and moreover, as I also observed, did
not appear at all disappointed.

One old *rangatira*, before whom a considerable portion of the payment had been
laid as his share of the spoil, gave it a slight
shove with his foot, expressive of refusal, and
said, "I will not accept any of the payment,
I will have the pakeha." I saw some of the
magnates present seemed greatly disappointed

N 2

at this, for I dare say they had expected to have the pakeha as well as the payment. But the old gentleman had regularly checkmated them by refusing to accept any payment, and being also a person of great respectability, *i.e.*, a good fighting man, with twenty more at his back, he was allowed to have his way, and thereby, in the opinion of all the natives present, making a far better thing of the land sale than any of them, though he had received no part of the payment.

I consequently was therefore a part, and by no means an inconsiderable one, of the payment for my own land ; but though now part and parcel of the property of the old *rangatira* aforementioned, a good deal of liberty was allowed me. The fact of my having become his pakeha made our respective relations and duties to each other about as follows—

Firstly.—At all times, places, and companies, my owner had the right to call me " his pakeha."

Secondly.—He had the general privilege of " pot-luck " whenever he chose to honour my establishment with a visit ; said pot-luck to be tumbled out to him on the ground before the house, he being far too great a man to eat out of plates or dishes, or any degenerate invention of that nature ; as, if he did, they would all become *tapu* and of no use to any one but himself, nor indeed to himself either, as he did not see the use of them.

Thirdly.—It was well understood that to avoid the unpleasant appearance of paying "black mail," and to keep up general kindly relations, my owner should from time to time make me small presents, and that in return I should make him presents of five or six times the value : all this to be done as if arising from mutual love and kindness, and not the slightest allusion to be ever made to the relative value of the gifts on either side, (an important article).

Fourthly.—It was to be a *sine quâ non* that I must purchase everything the chief or his family had to sell, whether I wanted them or not, and give the highest market price, or rather more. (Another very important article.)

Fifthly.—The chief's own particular pipe never to be allowed to become extinguished for want of the needful supply of tobacco.

Sixthly.—All desirable jobs of work, and all advantages of all kinds, to be offered first to the family of my *rangatira* before letting

anyone else have them; payment for same
to be about 25 per cent. more than to anyone else, exclusive of a *douceur* to the chief
himself because he did not work.

In return for these duties and customs,
well and truly performed on my part, the
chief was understood to—

Firstly.—Stick up for me in a general way,
and not let me be bullied or imposed upon by
any one but himself, as far as he was able to
prevent it.

Secondly.—In case of me being plundered
or maltreated by any powerful marauder, it
was the duty of my chief to come in hot haste
with all his family, armed to the teeth, to my
rescue, after all was over, and when it was too
late to be of any service. He was also bound
on such occasions to make a great noise,
dance the war dance, and fire muskets, (I
finding the powder,) and to declare loudly
what he would have done had he only been in
time. I, of course, on such occasions, for
my own dignity, and in consideration of the
spirited conduct of my friends, was bound to
order two or three fat pigs to be killed, and
lots of potatoes to be served out to the
"army," who were always expected to be
starving, as a general rule. A distribution of

tobacco, in the way of largess, was also a necessity of the case.

Thirdly.—In case of my losing anything of consequence by theft—a thing which, as a veracious pakeha, I am bound to say, seldom happened ; the natives in those days being, as I have already mentioned, a very law-observing people, (the law of *muru*,) had, indeed, little occasion to steal, the above-named law answering their purposes in a general way much better, and helping them pretty certainly to any little matter they coveted ; yet, as there are exceptions to all rules, theft would sometimes be committed ; and then, as I was saying, it became the bounden duty of my *rangatira* to get the stolen article back if he was able, and keep it for himself for his trouble, unless I gave him something of more value in lieu thereof.

Under the above regulations things went on pleasantly enough, the chief being restrained, by public opinion and the danger of the pakeha running away, from pushing his prerogative to the utmost limit ; and the pakeha, on the other hand, making the commonalty pay for the indirect taxation he was subjected to ; so that in general, after ten or fifteen years' residence, he would not be much poorer than when he arrived, unless, indeed, some unluckly accident happened, such as pakehas were liable to sometimes in the good old times.

Mentioning "public opinion" as a restraint on the chiefs' acquisitiveness, I must explain that a chief possessing a pakeha was much envied by his neighbours, who, in consequence, took every opportunity of scandalising him, and blaming him for any rough plucking process he might submit the said pakeha to; and should he, by any awkward handling of this sort, cause the pakeha at last to run for it, the chief would never hear the end of it from his own family and connections, pakehas being, in those glorious old times, considered to be geese who laid golden eggs, and it would be held to be the very extreme of foolishness and bad policy either to kill them, or, by too rough handling, to cause them to fly away.

On the other hand, should the pakeha fail in a culpable manner in the performance of his duties, though he would not, as a rule, be subjected to any stated punishment, he would soon begin to find a most unaccountable train of accidents and all sorts of unpleasant occurrences happening, enough, in the aggregate, to drive Job himself out of his wits ; and, moreover, he would *get a bad name*, which, though he removed, would follow him from one end of the island to the other, and effectually prevent him having the slightest chance of doing any good,—that is, holding his own in the country, as the natives, wherever he went, would consider him a person out of whom the most was to be made at once, as he was not to be depended on as a source of permanent revenue. I have known several industrious, active, and sober pakeha who never could do any good, and whose life, for a long series of years, was a mere train of mishaps, till at last they were reduced to extreme poverty, merely from having, in their first dealings with the natives, got a bad name, in consequence of not having been able to understand clearly the beauty of the set of regulations I have just mentioned, and from an inability to make them work smoothly. The bad name I have mentioned was short and expressive ; wherever they went, there would be sure to be some one who would introduce them to their new acquaintances as " a pakeha *pakeke*,"—a hard pakeha ; " a pakeha *taehae*"—a miser ; or, to sum up all, " a pakeha *kino*."

The chief who claimed me was a good

specimen of the Maori *rangatira*. He was a very old man, and had fought the French when Marion, the French circumnavigator, was killed. He had killed a Frenchman himself, and carried his thighs and legs many miles as a *bonne bouche* for his friends at home at the pa. This old gentleman was not head of his tribe. He was a man of good family, related to several high chiefs. He was head of a strong family, or *hapu*, which mustered a considerable number of fighting men, all his near relations. He had been himself a most celebrated fighting man, and a war chief; and was altogether a highly respectable person, and of great weight in the councils of the tribe. I may say I was fortunate in having been appropriated by this old patrician. He gave me very little trouble; did not press his rights and privileges too forcibly on my notice, and in fact behaved in all respects towards me in so liberal and friendly a manner, that before long I began to have a very sincere regard for him, and he to take a sort of paternal interest in me, which was both gratifying to observe, and also extremely comical sometimes, when he, out of real anxiety to see me a perfectly accomplished *rangatira*, would lecture on good manners, etiquette, and the use of the spear. He was, indeed, a model of a *rangatira*, and well worth being described. He was a little man, with a high massive head, and remarkably high square forehead, on which the tattooer had exhausted his art. Though, as I have said, of a great age, he was still nimble and active. He had evidently been one of those tough active men, who, though small in stature, are a match for any one. There was in my old friend's eyes a sort of dull fiery appearance, which, when anything excited him, or when he recounted some of those numerous battles, onslaughts, massacres, or stormings, in which all the active part of his life had been spent, actually seemed to blaze up and give forth real fire. His breast was covered with spear wounds, and he also had two very severe spear wounds on his head; but he boasted that no single man had ever been able to touch him with the point of a spear. It was in grand *melées*, where he would have sometimes six or eight antagonists, that he had received these wounds. He was a great general, and I have heard him criticise closely the order and conduct of every battle of consequence which had been fought for fifty years before my arrival in the country. On these occasions the old "martialist" would draw on the sand the plan of the battle he was criticising and describing; and, in the course of time I began to perceive that, before the introduction of the musket, the art of war had been brought to great perfection by the natives : and that, when large numbers were engaged in a pitched battle, the order of battle resembled, in a most striking manner, some of the most approved orders of battle of the ancients. Since the introduction of fire-arms the natives have entirely altered their tactics, and adopted a system better adapted to the new weapon and the nature of the country.

My old friend had a great hatred for the musket. He said that in battles fought with the musket there were never so many men killed as when, in his young days, men fought hand to hand with the spear ; when a good warrior would kill six, eight, ten, or even twenty men in a single fight ; for when once the enemy broke and commenced to run, the combatants being so close together, a fast runner would knock a dozen on the head in a short time ; and the great aim of these fast-running warriors, of whom my old friend had been one, was to chase straight on and never stop, only striking one blow at one man, so as to cripple him, so that those behind should be sure to overtake and finish him. It was not uncommon for one man, strong and swift of foot, when the enemy were fairly routed, to stab with a light spear ten or a dozen men in such a way as to ensure their being overtaken and killed. On one occasion of this kind my old tutor had the misfortune to stab a running man in the back. He did it of course scientifically, so as to stop his running, and as he passed him by he perceived it was his wife's brother. He was finished immediately by the men close behind. I should have said the man was a brother of one of my friend's four wives, which being the case, I dare say he had a sufficient number of brothers-in-law to afford to kill one now and then. A worse mishap, however, occurred to him on another occasion. He was returning from a successful expedition from the south, (in the course of which, by-the-bye, he and his men killed and cooked several men of the enemy in Shortland-crescent, and forced three others to jump over a cliff which is I think now called Soldier's-point), when off the Mahurangi a smoke was seen rising from amongst the trees near the beach. They at once concluded that it came from the fires of people belonging to that part of the country, and who they considered as game; they therefore waited till night, concealing their canoes behind some rocks, and when it became dark landed ; they then divided into two parties, took the supposed enemy completely by surprise, attacked, rushing upon them from two opposite directions at once. My *rangatira*, dashing furiously among them, and—as I can well suppose—those eyes of his flashing fire, had the happiness of once again killing the first man, and being authorised to shout "*Ki au te mataika!*" A few more blows, the parties recognise each other: they are friends!—men of the same tribe! Who is the last *mataika* slain by this famous warrior? Quick, bring a flaming brand—here he lies dead! Ha! It is his father!

Now an ancient knight of romance, under similar awkward circumstances, would probably have retired from public life, sought out some forest cave, where he would have hung up his armour, let his beard grow, flogged himself twice a day "regular," and lived on "pulse"—which I suppose means pea-soup—for the rest of his life. But my old *rangatira* and his companions had not a morsel of that sort of romance about them. The killing of

my friend's father was looked upon as a very
clever exploit in itself, though a very unlucky
one. So after having scolded one another
for some time, one party telling the other
they were served right for not keeping a better look out, and the other answering that
they should have been sure who they were
going to attack before making the onset,
they all held a *tangi* or lamentation for
the old warrior who had just received his
mittimus; and then killing a prisoner, who
they had brought in the canoes for fresh
provisions, they had a good feast ; after which
they returned all together to their own coun
try, taking the body of their lamented relative
along with them. This happened many years
before I came to the country, and when my
rangatira was one of the most famous fighting men in his tribe.

This Maori *rangatira*, who I am describing
had passed his whole life, with but little inter-
mission, in a scene of battle, murder, and
blood-thirsty atrocities of the most terrific
description, mixed with actions of the most
heroic courage, self-sacrifice, and chivalric
daring, as leaves one perfectly astounded to
find them the deeds of one and the same
people—one day doing acts which had they

been performed in ancient Greece would have immortalised the actors, and the next committing barbarities too horrible for relation, and almost incredible.

The effect of a life of this kind was observable, plainly enough, in my friend. He was utterly devoid of what weak mortals call "compassion." He seemed to have no more feeling for the pain, tortures, or death of others than a stone. Should one of his family be dying or wounded, he merely felt it as the loss of one fighting man. As for the death of a woman or any non-combatant, he did not feel it at all, though the person might have suffered horrid tortures; indeed I have seen him scolding severely a fine young man, his near relative, when actually expiring, for being such a fool as to blow himself up by accident, and deprive his family of a fighting man. The last words the dying man heard were these :—" It serves you right. There you are, looking very like a burnt stick ! It serves you right—a burnt stick ! Serves you right !" It really *was* vexatious. A fine stout young fellow to be wasted in that way. As for fear, I saw one or two instances to prove he knew very little about it ; and, indeed, to be killed in battle, seemed to him a

natural death, and he was always grumbling
that the young men thought of nothing but
trading : and whenever he proposed to them
to take him where he might have a final
battle *(he riri wakamutunga)*, where he might
escape dying of old age, they always kept
saying, " Wait till we get more muskets," or
" more gunpowder," or more something or
another, " as if men could not be killed without muskets ! " He was not cruel either ; he
was only unfeeling. He had been guilty, it is
true, in his time, of what we would call terrific
atrocities to his prisoners, which he calmly and
calculatingly perpetrated as *utu* or retaliation for similar barbarities committed by
them or their tribe. And here I must re-
tract the word guilty, which I see I have
written inadvertently, for according to the
morals and principles of the people of whom
he was one, and of the time to which he belonged, and the training he had received, so
far from being guilty, he did a praiseworthy,
glorious, and public-spirited action when he
opened the jugular vein of a bound captive
and sucked huge draughts of his blood. To
say the truth he was a very nice old man, and
I liked him very much. It would, not, however, be advisable to put him in a passion ; not

o

much good would be likely to arise from it, as indeed I could show by one or two very striking instances which came under my notice, though to say the truth he was not easily put out of temper. He had one great moral rule,—it was indeed his rule of life,—he held that every man had a right to do every-thing and anything he chose, provided he was able and willing to stand the consequences, though he thought some men fools for trying to do things which they could not carry out pleasantly, and which ended in getting them baked. I once hinted to him that, should every one reduce these principles to practice, he himself might find it awkward, particularly as he had so many mortal enemies. To which he replied, with a look which seemed to pity my ignorance, that every one *did* practice this rule to the best of their abilities, but that some were not so able as others; and that as for his enemies, he should take care they never surprised *him*; a surprise being, indeed, the only thing he seemed to have any fear at all of. In truth he had occasion to look out sharp; he never was known to sleep more than three or four nights in the same place, and often, when there were ill omens, he would not sleep in a house at all, or two nights following in one place, for a month together, and I never saw him without both spear and tomahawk, and ready to defend himself at a second's notice, a state of preparation perfectly necessary, for though in his own country and surrounded by his tribe, his death would have been such a triumph for hundreds, not of distant enemies, but of people within a day's journey, that none could tell at what moment some stout young fellow in search of *utu* and a " *ingoa toa* " (a warlike reputation) might rush upon him, determined to have his head or leave his own. The old buck himself had, indeed, performed several exploits of this nature, the last of which occurred just at the time I came into the country, but before I had the advantage of his acquaintance. His tribe were at war with some people at the distance of about a day's journey. One of their villages was on the border of a dense forest. My *rangatira*, then a very old man, started off alone, and without saying a word to any one, took his way through the forest which extended the whole way between his village and the enemy, crept like a lizard into the enemy's village, and then, shouting his war cry, dashed amongst a number of people he saw sitting together on the ground, and who little expected such a salute. In a minute he had run three men and one woman through the body, received five dangerous spear-wounds himself, and escaped to the forest, and finally got safe home to his own country and people. Truly my old *rangatira* was a man of a thousand,—a model *rangatira*. This exploit, if possible, added to his reputation, and every one said his *mana* would never decline. The enemy had been panic stricken, thinking a whole tribe were upon them, and fled like a flock of sheep, except the three men who were killed. They all attacked my old chief at once, and were all disposed of in less than a minute, after, as I have said, giving him five desperate wounds. The woman was just "stuck," as a matter of course, as she came in his way.

The natives are unanimous in affirming that they were much more numerous, in former times, than they are now, and I am convinced that such was the case, for the following reasons. The old hill forts are many of them so large that an amount of labour must have been expended in trenching, terracing, and fencing them, and all without iron tools, which increased the difficulty a hundred-fold, which must have required a vastly greater population to accomplish than can be now found in the surrounding districts. These forts were also of such an extent that, taking into consideration the system of attack and defence used necessarily in those times, they would have been utterly untenable unless held by at least ten times the number of men the whole surrounding districts, for two or three days' journey, can produce; and yet, when we remember that in those times of constant war, being the two centuries preceding the arrival of the Europeans, the natives always, as a rule, slept in these hill forts with closed gates, bridges over trenches removed, and ladders of terraces drawn up, we must come to the conclusion that the inhabitants of the fort, though so numerous, were merely the population of the country in the close vicinity. Now from the top of one of these pointed, trenched, and terraced hills, I have counted twenty others, all of equally large dimensions, and all within a distance, in every direction, of fifteen to twenty miles; and native tradition affirms that each of these hills was the stronghold of a separate *hapu* or clan, bearing its distinctive name. There is also the most unmistakeable evidence that vast tracks of country, which have lain wild time out of mind, were once fully cultivated. The ditches for draining the land are still traceable, and large pits are to be seen in hundreds, on the tops of the dry hills, all over the northern part of the North Island, in which the *kumera* were once stored; and these pits are, in the greatest number, found in the centre of great open tracts of uncultivated country, where a rat in the present day would hardly find subsistence. The old drains, and the peculiar growth of the timber, mark clearly the extent of these ancient cultivations. It is also very observable that large tracts of very inferior land have been in cultivation, which would lead to the inference that either the population was pretty nearly proportioned to the extent of available land, or that the tracts of inferior land were cultivated merely because they were not too far removed from the fort; for the shape of the hill, and its capability of defence and facility of fortification, was of more consequence than the fertility of the surrounding country. These *kumera* pits, being dug generally in the stiff clay on the hill tops, have, in most cases, retained their shape perfectly, and many seem as fresh and new as if they had been dug but a few years. They are oblong in shape, with the sides regularly sloped. Many collections of these provision stores have outlived Maori tradition, and the natives can only conjecture who they belonged to. Out of the centre of one of them which I have seen, there is now growing a kauri tree one hundred and twenty feet high, and out of another a large totara. The outline of these pits· is as perfect as the day they were dug, and the sides have not fallen in in the slightest degree, from which perhaps they have been preserved by the absence of frost, as well as by a beautiful coating of moss, by which they are every-where covered. The pit in which the kauri grew, had been partially filled up by the scaling off of the bark of the tree, which, falling off in patches, as it is constantly doing, had raised a mound of decaying bark round the root of the tree.

Another evidence of a very large number of people having once inhabited these hill forts is the number of houses they contained. Every native house, it appears, in former times as in the present, had a fire-place composed of four flat stones or flags sunk on their edges into the ground, so as to form an oblong case or trunk, in which at night a fire to heat the house was made. Now, in two of the largest hill forts I have examined, though for ages no vestige of a house had been seen, there remained the fire-places—the four stones projecting like an oblong box slightly over the ground—and from their position and number denoting clearly that, large as the circumference of the huge volcanic hill was which formed the fortress, the number of families inhabiting it necessitated the strictest economy of room. The houses had been arranged in streets, or double rows, with a path between them, except in places where there had been only room on a terrace for a single row. The distances between the fire-places proved that the houses in the rows must have been as close together as it was possible to build them, and every spot, from the foot to the hill top, not required and specially planned for defensive purposes, had been built on in this regular manner. Even the small flat top, sixty yards long by forty wide,—the citadel,—on which the greatest care and labour had been bestowed to render it difficult of access, had been as full of houses as it could hold, leaving a small space all round the precipitous bank for the defenders to stand on.

These little fire-places, and the scarped and terraced conical hills, are the only mark the Maori of ancient times have left of their existence. And I have reasons for believing that this country has been inhabited from a more remote period by far than is generally supposed. These reasons I found upon the dialect of the Maori language spoken by the Maori of New Zealand, as well as on many other circumstances.

We may easily imagine that a hill of this kind, covered from bottom to top with houses thatched and built of reeds, rushes, and raupo, would be a mere mass of combustible matter, and such indeed was the case. When an enemy attacked one of these places a common practice was to shower red-hot stones from slings into the place, which, sinking into the dry thatch of the houses, would cause a general conflagration. Should this once occur the place was sure to be taken, and this mode of attack was much feared; all hands not engaged at the outer defences, and all women and non-combatants, were employed guarding against this danger, and pouring water out of calabashes on every smoke that appeared. The natives also practised both mining and escalade in attacking a hill fort.

The natives attribute their decrease in umbers, before the arrival of the Europeans, to war and sickness, disease possibly arising from the destruction of food and the forced neglect of cultivation caused by the constant and furious wars which devastated the country for a long period before the arrival of the Europeans, in such a manner that the natives at last believed that a constant state of warfare was the natural condition of life, and their sentiments, feelings, and maxims became gradually formed on this belief. Nothing was so valuable or respectable as strength and courage, and to acquire property by war and plunder more honourable and also more desirable than by labour. Cannibalism was glorious. The island was a pandemonium.

> A rugged wight, the worst of brutes, was man ;
> On his own wretched kind he ruthless prey'd.
> The strongest then the weakest overran,
> In every country mighty robbers sway'd,
> And guile and ruffian force was all their trade.

Since the arrival of the Europeans the decrease of the natives has also been rapid. In that part of the country where I have had means of accurate observation, they have decreased in number since my arrival rather more than one-third. I have, however, observed that this decrease has for the last ten years been very considerably checked, though I do not believe this improvement is general through the country, or even permanent where I have observed it.

The first grand cause of the decrease of the natives since the arrival of the Europeans is the musket. The nature of the ancient Maori weapons prompted them to seek out vantage ground, and to take up positions on precipitous hill tops, and make those high, dry, airy situations their regular fixed residences. Their ordinary course of life, when not engaged in warfare, was regular, and not necessarily unhealthy. Their labour, though constant in one shape or other, and compelled by necessity, was not too heavy. In the morning, but not early, they descended from the hill pa to the cultivations in the low ground; they went in a body, armed like men going to battle, the spear or club in one hand, and the agricultural instrument in the other. The women followed. Long before night (it was counted unlucky to work till dark) they returned to the hill with a reversed order, the women now, and slaves, and lads, bearing fuel and water for the night, in front; they also bore probably heavy loads of *kumera* or other provisions. . In the time of year when the crops did not call for their attention, when they were planted and growing, then the whole tribe would remove to some fortified hill, at the side of some river, or on the coast, where they would pass months, fishing, making nets, clubs, spears, and implements of various descriptions; the women, in all spare time, making mats for clothing, or baskets to carry the crop of *kumera* in, when fit to dig. There was very little idleness; and to be called " lazy " was a great reproach.   It is to be observed that for several months the crops could be left thus unguarded with perfect safety, for the Maori, as a general rule, never destroyed growing crops or attacked their owners in a regular manner until the crops were nearly at full perfection, so that they might afford subsistence to the invaders, and consequently the end of the summer all over the country was a time of universal preparation for battle, either offensive or defensive, the crops then being near maturity.

Now when the natives became generally armed with the musket they at once abandoned the hills, and, to save themselves the great labour and inconvenience occasioned by the necessity of continually carrying provisions, fuel, and water to these precipitous hill-castles—which would be also, as a matter of necessity, at some inconvenient distance from at least some part of the extensive cultivations—descended to the low lands, and there, in the centre of the cultivations, erected a new kind of fortification adapted to the capabilities of the new weapon. *This* was their destruction. There in mere swamps they built their oven-like houses, where the water even in summer sprung with the pressure of the foot, and where in winter the houses were often completely flooded. There, lying on the spongy soil, on beds of rushes which rotted under them—in little, low, dens of houses, or kennels, heated like ovens at night and dripping with damp in the day—full of noxious exhalations from the damp soil, and impossible to ventilate—they were cut off by disease in a manner absolutely frightful. No advice would they take ; they could not *see* the enemy which killed them, and therefore could not believe the Europeans who pointed out the cause of their destruction.

This change of residence was universal and everywhere followed by the same consequences, more or less marked ; the strongest men were cut off and but few children were reared. And even now, after the dreadful experience they have had, and all the continual remonstrances of their pakeha friends, they take but very little more precaution in choosing sites for their houses than at first; and when a native village or a native house happens to be in a dry healthy situation, it is often more the effect of accident than design.

Twenty years ago a *hapu*, in number just forty persons, removed their *kainga* from a dry healthy position, to the edge of a *raupo* swamp. I happened to be at the place a short time after the removal, and with me there was a medical gentleman who was travelling through the country. In creeping into one of the houses (the chief's) through the low door, I was obliged to put both my hands to the ground; they both sunk into the swampy soil, making holes which immediately filled with water. The chief and his family were lying on the ground on rushes, and a fire was burning, which made the little den, not in the highest place more than five feet high, feel like an oven. I called the attention of my friend to the state of this place called a "house." He merely said, " *men* cannot live here." Eight years from that day the whole *hapu* were extinct ; but, as I remember, two persons were shot for bewitching them and causing their deaths.

Many other causes combined at the same time to work the destruction of the natives. Next to the change of residence from the high and healthy hill forts to the low grounds, was the hardship, over-labour, exposure, and half-starvation, to which they submitted themselves — firstly, to procure these very muskets which enabled them to make the fatal change of residence, and afterwards to procure the highly and justly valued iron implements of the Europeans. When we reflect that a ton of cleaned flax was the price paid for two muskets, and at an earlier date for one musket, we can see at once the dreadful exertion necessary to obtain it. But supposing a man to get a musket for half a ton of flax, another half ton would be required for ammunition ; and in consequence, as every man in a native *hapu*, of say a hundred men, was absolutely forced on pain of death to procure a musket and ammunition at any cost, and at the earliest possible moment, (for if they did not procure them extermination was their doom by the hands of those of their

countrymen who had), the effect was that
this small *hapu,* or clan, had to manufacture,
spurred by the penalty of death, in the shortest possible time, one hundred tons of flax,
scraped by hand with a shell, bit by bit,
morsel by morsel, half-quarter of an ounce
at a time.   Now as the natives, when undis-
turbed and labouring regularly at their cultivations, were never far removed from
necessity or scarcity of food, we may easily
imagine the distress and hardship caused
by this enormous imposition of extra labour.
They were obliged to neglect their crops in a
very serious degree, and for many months in
the year were in a half-starving condition,
working hard all the time in the flax swamps.
The insufficient food, over exertion, and un-
wholesome locality, killed them fast.   As for
the young children, they almost all died ; and
this state of things continued for many years:
for it was long after being supplied with arms
and ammunition before the natives could
purchase, by similar exertion, the various
agricultural implements, and other iron tools
so necessary to them ; and it must always
be remembered, if we wish to understand
the difficulties and over-labour the natives
were subjected to, that while undergoing this

immense extra toil, they were at the same
time obliged to maintain themselves by culti-
vating the ground with sharpened sticks, not
being able to afford to purchase iron implements in any useful quantity, till first the
great, pressing, paramount, want of muskets
and gunpowder had been supplied. Thus
continual excitement, over-work, and insufficient food, exposure, and unhealthy places of
residence, together with a general breaking
up of old habits of life, thinned their numbers.
European diseases also assisted, but not to
any very serious degree; till in the part of
the country in which, as I have before stated,
I have had means to observe with exactitude,
the natives have decreased in numbers over
one-third since I first saw them. That this rapid
decrease has been checked in some districts, I
am sure, and the cause is not a mystery. The
influx of Europeans has caused a competition
in trading, which enables them to get the
highest value for the produce of their labour,
and at the same time opened to them a hundred new lines of industry, and also afforded
them other opportunities of becoming possessed of property. They have not at all
improved these advantages as they might
have done; but are, nevertheless, as it were

in spite of themselves, on the whole, richer—
i.e., better clothed, fed, and in some degree
lodged, than in past years; and I see the
plough now running where I once saw the
rude pointed stick poking the ground. I do
not, however, believe that this improvement
exists in more than one or two districts in any
remarkable degree, nor do I think it will be
permanent where it does exist, insomuch as I
have said that the improvement is not the
result of providence, economy, or industry,
but of a train of temporary circumstances
favourable to the natives; but which, if un-
improved, as they most probably will be, will
end in no permanent good result.

CHAPTER XIV.

FROM the years 1822 to 1826, the vessels trading for flax had, when at anchor, boarding nettings up to the tops. All the crew were armed, and, as a standing rule, not more than five natives, on any pretence, allowed on board at one time. Trading for flax in those days was to be undertaken by a man who had his wits about him ; and an old flax trader of those days, with his 150 ton schooner " out of Sydney," cruising all round the coast of New Zealand, picking up his five tons at one port, ten at another, twenty at another, and so on, had questions, commercial, diplomatic, and military, to solve every day, that would drive all the " native department," with the minister at their head, clean out of their senses. Talk to me of the "native difficulty"—pooh ! I think it was in 1822 that an old friend of mine bought, at Kawhia, a woman who was just going to be baked.   He gave a cartridge-box full of cartridges for her, which was a great deal more than she was really worth; but humanity does not stick at trifles.   He took her back to her friends at Taranaki, from whence she had been taken, and her friends there gave him at once two tons of flax and eighteen pigs, and asked him to remain a few days longer till they should collect a still larger present in return for his kindness ; but, as he found out their intention was to take the schooner, and knock himself and crew on the head, he made off in the night.   But he maintains, to this day, that " virtue is its own reward "—" at least 'tis so at Taranaki."   Virtue, however, must have been on a visit to some other country, (she *does* go out sometimes,) when I saw and heard a British subject, a slave to some natives on the West Coast, begging hard for somebody to buy him.   The price asked was one musket, but the only person on board the vessel possessing those articles, preferred to invest in a different commodity.   The consequence was, that the above-mentioned unit of the great British nation lived, and (" Rule Britannia" to the contrary notwithstanding) died a slave ; but whether he was buried, deponent sayeth not.

My old *rangatira* at last began to show signs that his time to leave this world of care was approaching. He had arrived at a great age, and a rapid and general breaking up of his strength became plainly observable. He often grumbled that men should grow old, and oftener that no great war broke out in which he might make a final display, and die with *eclât*. The last two years of his life were spent almost entirely at my house, which, however, he never entered. He would sit whole days on a fallen puriri near the house, with his spear sticking up beside him, and speaking to no one, but sometimes humming in a low droning tone some old ditty which no one knew the meaning of but himself, and at night he would disappear to some of the numerous nests or little sheds he had around the place. In summer he would roll himself in his blanket and sleep anywhere, but no one could tell exactly where. In the hot days of summer, when his blood I suppose got a little warm, he would sometimes become talkative, and recount the exploits of his youth. As he warmed to the subject he would seize his spear and go through all the incidents of some famous combat, repeating every thrust, blow, and parry as they actually

occurred, and going through as much exertion as if he was really and truly fighting
for his life. He used to go through these
pantomimic labours as a duty whenever he had
an assemblage of the young men of the tribe
around him, to whom, as well as to myself, he
was most anxious to communicate that which
he considered the most valuable of all knowledge, a correct idea of the uses of the spear, a
weapon he really used in a most graceful and
scientific manner ; but he would ignore the
fact that " Young New Zealand" had laid
down the weapon for ever, and already ma-
tured a new system of warfare adapted to their
new weapons, and only listened to his lectures
out of respect to himself and not for his
science. At last this old lion was taken
seriously ill and removed permanently to the
village, and one evening a smart handsome
lad, of about twelve years of age, came to tell
me that his *tupuna* was dying, and had said
he would "go" to-morrow, and had sent for
me to see him before he died. The boy also
added that the tribe were *ka poto*, or assembled, to the last man around the dying
chief. I must here mention that, though this
old *rangatira* was not the head of his tribe,
he had been for about half a century the

recognised war chief of almost all the sections or *hapu* of a very numerous and warlike *iwi* or tribe, who had now assembled from all their distant villages and pas to see him die. I could not, of course, neglect the invitation, so at daylight next morning I started on foot for the native village, which I, on my arrival about mid-day, found crowded by a great assemblage of natives. I was saluted by the usual *haere mai!* and a volley of musketry, and I at once perceived that, out of respect to my old owner, the whole tribe from far and near, hundreds of whom I had never seen, considered it necessary to make much of me,—at least for that day,—and I found myself consequently at once in the position of a "personage." "Here comes the pakeha!—*his* pakeha!—make way for the pakeha!—kill those dogs that are barking at the pakeha!" Bang! bang! Here a double barrel nearly blew my cap off by way of salute. I did for a moment think my head was off. I, however, being quite *au fait* in Maori etiquette by this time, thanks to the instructions and example of my old friend, fixed my eyes with a vacant expression looking only straight before me, recognised nobody, and took notice of nothing, not even

the muskets fired under my nose or close to
my back at every step, and each, from having
four or five charges of powder, making a report like a cannon. On I stalked, looking
neither to the right or the left, with my spear
walking-staff in my hand, to where I saw a
great crowd, and where I of course knew the
dying man was. I walked straight on, not
even pretending to see the crowd, as was
"correct" under the circumstances; I being
supposed to be entranced by the one absorb-
ing thought of seeing "mataora," or once
more in life my *rangatira*. The crowd
divided as I came up, and closed again
behind me as I stood in the front rank
before the old chief, motionless, and, as in
duty bound, trying to look the image of mute
despair, which I flatter myself I did to the
satisfaction of all parties. The old man I
saw at once was at his last hour. He had
dwindled to a mere skeleton. No food of any
kind had been prepared for or offered to him
for three days; as he was dying it was of
course considered unnecessary. At his right
side lay his spear, tomahawk, and musket. (I
never saw him with the musket in his hand
all the time I knew him.) Over him was
hanging his greenstone *mere*, and at his left

side, close, and touching him, sat a stout athletic savage, with a countenance disgustingly expressive of cunning and ferocity, and who, as he stealthily marked me from the corner of his eye, I recognised as one of those limbs of Satan, a Maori *tohunga*. The old man was propped up in a reclining position, his face towards the assembled tribe, who were all there waiting to catch his last words. I stood before him and I thought I perceived he recognised me. Still all was silence, and for a full half hour we all stood there, waiting patiently for the closing scene. Once or twice the *tohunga* said to him in a very loud voice, "The tribe are assembled, you won't die silent?" At last, after about half-an-hour, he became restless, his eyes rolled from side to side, and he tried to speak, but failed. The circle of men closed nearer, and there was evidence of anxiety and expectation amongst them, but a dead silence was maintained. At last, suddenly without any apparent effort, and in a manner which startled me, the old man spoke clearly out, in the ringing metallic tone of voice for which he had been formerly so remarkable, particularly when excited. He spoke. "Hide my bones quickly where the enemy

may not find them : hide them at once."
He spoke again—"Oh my tribe, be brave !
be brave that you may live. Listen to the
words of my pakeha ; he will unfold the designs of his tribe." This was in allusion to a
very general belief amongst the natives at the
time, that the Europeans designed sooner or
later to exterminate them and take the country, a thing the old fellow had cross-ques-
tioned me about a thousand times ; and the
only way I could find to ease his mind was to
tell him that if ever I heard any such proposal
I would let him know, protesting at the same
time that no such intention existed. This notion
of the natives has since that time done much
harm, and will do more, for it is not yet quite
given up. He continued—" I give my *mere* to
my pakeha,"—" my two old wives will hang
themselves,"—(here a howl of assent from the
two old women in the rear rank)—"I am going ;
be brave, after I am gone." Here he began
to rave ; he fancied himself in some desperate
battle, for he began to call to celebrated comrades who had been dead forty or fifty years.
I remember every word—" Charge !" shouted
he—" Charge ! *Wata*, charge ! *Tara*, charge !
charge !" Then after a short pause—" Rescue !
rescue ! to my rescue ! *ahau ! ahau ! rescue !*"

The last cry for "rescue" was in such a pier-
cing tone of anguish and utter desperation,
that involuntarily I advanced a foot and hand,
as if starting to his assistance ; a movement,
as I found afterwards, not unnoticed by the
superstitious tribe.   At the same instant that
he gave the last despairing and most agonising
cry for "rescue," I saw his eyes actually blaze,
his square jaw locked, he set his teeth, and rose
nearly to a sitting position, and then fell back
dying.   He only murmured—"How sweet is
man's flesh," and then the gasping breath and
upturned eye announced the last moment.
The *tohunga* now bending close to the dying
man's ear, roared out "*Kai kotahi ki te ao!
Kia kotahi ki te ao !   Kia kotahi ki te po !*"
The poor savage was now, as I believe, past
hearing, and gasping his last.   "*Kai kotahi
ki te ao !*"—shouted the devil priest again in
his ear, and shaking his shoulder roughly
with his hand—"*Kia kotahi ki te ao !—Kia
kotahi ki te po!*   Then giving a significant
look to the surrounding hundreds of natives,
a roar of musketry burst forth.   *Kai kotahi ki
te ao!*   Thus in a din like pandemonium,
guns firing, women screaming, and the ac-
cursed *tohunga* shouting in his ear, died
"Lizard Skin," as good a fighting man as

ever worshipped force or trusted in the spear. His death on the whole was thought happy, for his last words were full of good omen :— "How sweet is man's flesh."

Next morning the body had disappeared. This was contrary to ordinary custom, but in accordance with the request of the old warrior. No one, even of his own tribe, knows where his body is concealed, but the two men who carried it off in the night. All I know is that it lies in a cave, with the spear and tomahawk beside it.

The two old wives were hanging by the neck from a scaffold at a short distance, which had been made to place potatoes on out of the reach of rats. The shrivelled old creatures were quite dead. I was for a moment forgetful of the "correct" thing, and called to an old chief, who was near, to cut them down. He said, in answer to my hurried call, "by-and-bye; it is too soon yet ; *they might recover.*" "Oh," said I, at once recalled to my sense of propriety, "I thought they had been hanging all night," and thus escaped the great risk of being thought a mere meddling pakeha. I now perceived the old chief was employed making a stretcher, or *kauhoa*, to carry the bodies on. At a short distance also were five old creatures of women, sitting in a row, crying, with their eyes fixed on the hanging objects, and everything was evidently going on *selon le regles.* I walked on. "*E tika ana,*" said I, to myself. "It's all right, I dare say."

The two young wives had also made a· desperate attempt in the night to hang themselves, but had been prevented by two young men, who, by some unaccountable accident, had come upon them just as they were stringing themselves up, and who, seeing that they were not actually "ordered for execution," by great exertion, and with the assistance of several female relations, who they called to their assistance, prevented them from killing themselves out of respect for their old lord. Perhaps it was to revenge themselves for this meddling interference that these two young women married the two young men before the year was out, and in consequence of which, and as a matter of course, they were robbed by the tribe of everything they had in the world, (which was not much,) except their arms. They also had to fight some half dozen duels each with spears, in which, however, no one was killed, and no more blood drawn than could be well spared. All this they went through with commendable resignation; and so, due respect having been paid to the memory of the old chief, and the appropriators of his widows duly punished according to law, further proceedings were stayed, and everything went on comfortably. And so the ·world goes round.

CHAPTER XV.

In the afternoon I went home musing on what I had heard and seen. "Surely," thought I, "if one half of the world does not know how the other half live, neither do they know how they die."

Some days after this a deputation arrived to deliver up my old friend's *mere*. It was a weapon of great *mana*, and was delivered with some little ceremony. I perceive now I have written this word *mana* several times, and think I may as well explain what it means. I think this the more necessary, as the word has been bandied about a good deal of late years, and meanings often attached to it by Europeans which are incorrect, but which the natives sometimes accept because it suits their purpose. This same word *mana* has several different meanings, and the difference between these diverse meanings is sometimes very great, and sometimes only a mere shade of meaning, though one very necessary to observe ; and it is, therefore, quite impossible to find any one single word in English, or in any other language that I have any acquaintance with, which will give the meaning of *mana*.   And, moreover, though I myself do know all the meanings and different shades of meaning, properly belonging to the word, I find a great difficulty in explaining them ; but as I have begun, the thing must be done.   It will also be a tough word disposed of to my hand, when I come to write my Maori dictionary, in a hundred volumes, which, if I begin soon, I hope to have finished before the Maori is a dead language.

Now then for *mana*. *Virtus, prestigé,* authority, good fortune, influence, sanctity, luck, are all words which, under certain conditions, give something near the meaning of *mana*, though not one of them give it exactly ; but before I am done, the reader shall have a reasonable notion (for a pakeha) of what it is.

Mana sometimes means a more than natural virtue or power attaching to some

person or thing, different from and independent of the ordinary natural conditions of
either, and capable of either increase or
diminution, both from known and unknown
causes The *mana* of a priest or *tohunga* is
proved by the truth of his predictions, as well
as the success of his incantations, *which same
incantations, performed by another person of
inferior mana, would have no effect.* Consequently, this description of *mana* is a virtue,
or more than natural or ordinary condition
attaching to the priest himself, and which he
may become possessed of and also lose without any volition of his own. When

"Apollo from his shrine,
No longer could divine,
The hollow steep of Delphos sadly leaving,"—

Then the oracle had lost its *mana*.

Then there is the doctors' *mana*. The
Maori doctors in the old times did not deal
much in "simples," but they administered
large doses of *mana*. Now when most of a
doctor's patients recovered, his *mana* was supposed to be in full feather ; but if, as will
happen sometimes to the best practitioners, a
number of patients should slip through his

Q

fingers *seriatim*, then his *mana* was suspected to be getting weak, and he would not be liable to be "knocked up" as frequently as formerly.

Mana in another sense is the accompaniment of power, but not the power itself; nor is it even in this sense exactly "authority," according to the strict meaning of that word, though it comes very near it. This is the chief's *mana*. Let him lose the power, and the *mana* is gone; but mind you do not translate *mana* as power; that won't do: they are two different things entirely. Of this nature also is the *mana* of a tribe; but this is not considered to be the supernatural kind of *mana*.

Then comes the *mana* of a warrior. Uninterrupted success in war proves it. It has a *slight* touch of the supernatural, but not much. Good fortune comes near the meaning, but is just a little too weak. The warrior's *mana* is just a little something more than bare good fortune; a severe defeat would shake it terribly; two or three in succession would show that it was gone: but before leaving him, some supernaturally ominous occurrence might be expected to take place, such as are said

to have happened before the deaths of Julius
Cæsar, Marcus Antonius, or Brutus. Let
not any one smile at my, even in the most
distant way, comparing the old Maori warriors with these illustrious Romans, for if
they do, I shall answer that some of the old
Maori *Toa* were thought as much of in *their*
world, as any Greek or Roman of old was in
his ; and, moreover, that it is my private
opinion, that if the best of them could only
have met my friend " Lizard Skin," in his
best days, and would take off his armour and
fight fair, that the aforesaid " Lizard Skin "
would have tickled him to his heart's content
with the point of his spear.

A fortress often assailed but never taken
has a *mana*, and one of a high description too.
The name of the fortress becomes a *pepeha*, a
war·boast or motto, and a war cry of encouragement or defiance, like the *slogan* of the
ancient Highlanders in Scotland.

A spear, a club, or a *mere*, may have a
mana, which in most cases means that it is a
lucky weapon which good fortune attends, if
the bearer minds what he is about ; but some
weapons of the old times had a stronger
mana than this, like the *mana* of the enchanted

weapons we read of in old romances or fairy tales. Let any one who likes give an English word for this kind of *mana*. I have done with it.

I had once a tame pig, which, before heavy rain, would always cut extraordinary capers and squeak like mad. Every pakeha said he was "weather-wise;" but all the Maori said it was a *"poaka whai mana,"* a pig possessed of *mana; it had more than natural powers* and could foretell rain.

If ever this talk about the good old times be printed and published, and every one buy it, and read it, and quote it, and believe every word in it, as they ought, seeing that every word is true, then it will be a *puka puka whai mana*, a book of *mana*; and I shall have a high opinion of the good sense and good taste of the New Zealand public.

When the law of England is the law of New Zealand, and the Queen's writ will run, then both the Queen and the law will have great *mana*; but I don't think either will ever happen, and so neither will have any *mana* of consequence.

If the reader has not some faint notion of *mana* by this time, I can't help it; I can't do

any better for him. I must confess I have
not pleased myself. Any European language
can be translated easily enough into any
other ; but to translate Maori into English is
much harder to do than is supposed by those
who do it every day with ease, but who do
not know their own language or any other
but Maori perfectly.

I am always blowing up " Young New
Zealand," and calling them " reading, riting,
rethmatiking" vagabonds, who will never
equal their fathers ; but I mean it all for
their own good —(poor things !)—like a father
scolding his children. But one *does* get
vexed sometimes. Their grandfathers, if they
had no backs, had at least good legs, but the
grandsons can't walk a day's journey to save
their lives : *they* must *ride*. The other day
I saw a young chap on a good horse : he had
a black hat and polished Wellingtons : his hat
was cocked knowingly to one side : he was
jogging along, with one hand jingling the
money in his pocket ; and may I never see
another war dance, if the hardened villain
was not whistling " Pop goes the weasel !"
What will all this end in ?

My only hope is in a handy way (to give

them their due) which they have with a *tupara;* and this is why I don't think the law will have much *mana* here in my time,—I mean the *pakeha* law ; for to say the worst of them, they are not yet so far demoralised as to stand any nonsense of that kind, which is a comfort to think of. I am a loyal subject to Queen Victoria, but I am also a member of a Maori tribe ; and I hope I may never see this country so enslaved and tamed that a single rascally policeman, with nothing but a bit of paper in his hand, can come and take a *rangatira* away from the middle of his *hapu*, and have him hanged for something of no consequence at all, except that it is against the law. What would old " Lizard Skin " say to it ? His grandson certainly is now a magistrate, and if anything is stolen from a pakeha, he will get it back, *if he can*, and won't stick to it, because he gets a salary in lieu thereof; but he has told me certain matters in confidence, and which I therefore cannot disclose. I can only hint there was something said about the law, and driving the pakeha into the sea.

I must not trust myself to write on these matters. I get so confused, I feel just as if

I was two different persons at the same time. Sometimes I find myself thinking on the Maori side, and then just afterwards wondering if "we" can lick the Maori, and set the law upon its legs, which is the only way to do it. I therefore hope the reader will make allowance for any little apparent inconsistency in my ideas, as I really cannot help it.

I belong to both parties, and I don't care a straw which wins ; but I am sure we shall have fighting. Men *must* fight ; or else what are they made for ? Twenty years ago, when I heard military men talking of "marching through New Zealand with fifty men," I was called a fool because I said they could not do it with five hundred. Now I am also thought foolish by civilians, because I say we can conquer New Zealand with our present available means, if we set the right way about it, (which we won't). So hurrah again for the Maori ! We shall drive the pakeha into the sea, and send the law after them ! If we can do it, we are right ; and if the pakeha beat us, *they* will be right too. God save the Queen !

So now, my Maori tribe, and also my

pakeha countrymen, I shall conclude this book with good advice ; and be sure you take notice ; it is given to both parties. It is a sentence from the last speech of old " Lizard Skin." It is to you both. " Be brave, that you may live."

VERBUM SAPIENTIE.

GLOSSARY.

GLOSSARY.

PAGE 2.

No hea—Literally, from whence? Often used as a negative answer to an enquiry, in which case the words mean that the thing enquired for is not, or in fact is nowhere.

PAGE 3.

Mana—As the meaning of this word is explained in the course of the narrative, it is only necessary to say that in the sense in which it is used here, it means dominion or authority.

Tangi – A dirge, or song of lamentation for the dead. It was the custom for the mourners, when singing the *tangi*, to cut themselves severely on the face, breast, and arms, with sharp flints and shells, in token of their grief. This custom is still practised, though in a mitigated form. In past times, the mourners cut themselves dreadfully, and covered themselves with blood from head to feet. See a description of a *tangi* further on.

PAGE 4.

Pakeha – An Englishman ; a foreigner.

PAGE 13.

Tupara—A double gun ; an article, in the old times, valued by the natives above all other earthly riches.

PAGE 14.

Hahunga—A *hahunga* was a funeral ceremony, at which the natives usually assembled in great numbers, and during which "baked meats" were disposed of with far less economy than Hamlet gives us to suppose was observed "in Denmark."

Kainga—A native town, or village : their principal head quarters.

PAGE 16.

Haere mai ! &c.—Sufficiently explained as the native call of welcome. It is literally an invitation to advance.

PAGE 19.

Tutua—A low, worthless, and, above all, a *poor*, fellow—a " nobody."

A pakeha tutua—A mean *poor* European.

E aha te pai ?—What is the good (or use) of him ? Said in contempt.

PAGE 22.

Rangatira—A chief, a gentleman, a warrior. *Rangatira pakeha*—A foreigner who is a gentleman (not a *tutua*, or nobody, as described above), a *rich* foreigner.

Taonga—Goods ; property.

Page 26.

Mere ponamu—A native weapon made of a rare green stone, and much valued by the natives.

Page 28.

Taniwha—A sea monster : more fully described further on.
Utu—Revenge, or satisfaction ; also payment.

Page 32.

Tino tangata—A "good man," in the language of the prize-ring ; a warrior ; or literally, a very, or perfect man.

Page 45.

Taua—A war party : or war expedition.

Page 58.

Tena koutou ; or Tenara ko koutou—The Maori form of salutation, equivalent to our " How do you do ?"

Page 63.

Na ! Na ! mate rawa !—This is the battle cry by which a warrior proclaims, exultingly and tauntingly, the death of one of the enemy.

Page 78.

Torere.—An unfathomable cave, or pit, in the rocky mountains, where the bones of the dead, after remaining a certain time in the first burying place, are removed to and thrown in, and so finally disposed of.

Page 102.

Eaha mau—What's that to you.

Page 166.

Jacky Poto.—Short Jack ; or Stumpy Jack.

PAGE 167.

Tu ngarahu.—This is a muster, or review, made to ascertain the numbers and condition of a native force ; generally made before the starting of an expedition. It is, also, often held as a military spectacle, or exhibition, of the force of a tribe when they happen to be visited by strangers of importance : the war dance is gone through on these occasions, and speeches declaratory of war, or welcome, as the case may be, made to the visitors. The " review of the Taniwha," witnessed by the Ngati Kuri, was possibly a herd of sea lions, or sea elephants ; animals scarcely ever seen on the coast of that part of New Zealand, and, therefore, from their strange and hideous appearance, at once set down as an army of Taniwha. One man only was, at the defeat of the Ngati Kuri, on Motiti, rescued to tell the tale.

PAGE 168.

Bare Motiti.—The island of Motiti is often called " *Motiti wahie kore,*" as descriptive of the want of timber, or bareness of the island. A more fiercely contested battle, perhaps, was never fought than that on Motiti, in which the Ngati Kuri were destroyed.

PAGE 190.

Ki au te matuika—I have the *matuika.* The first man killed in a battle was called the *matuika.* To kill the *matuika,* or first man, was counted a very high honor, and the most extraordinary exertions were made to obtain it. The writer once saw a young warrior, when rushing with his tribe against the enemy, rendered almost frantic by perceiving that another section of the tribe would, in spite of all his efforts, be engaged first, and gain the honor of killing the *mataika*. In this emergency he, as he rushed on, cut down with a furious blow of his tomahawk, a sapling which stood in his way, and gave the cry which claims the *mataika*. After the battle the circumstances of this question in Maori chivalry having been fully considered by the elder warriors, it was decided that the sapling tree should, in this case, be held to be the true *mataika*, and that the young man who cut it down should always claim, without question, to have killed, or as the natives say, "caught," the *mataika* of that battle.

PAGE 195.

Toa—A warrior of preëminant courage ; a hero.

PAGE 219.

Kia Kotahi ki te ao ! Kia kotahi ki te po !—A close translation would not give the meaning to the English reader. By these words the dying person is conjured to cling to life, but as they are never spoken until the person to whom they are addressed is actually expiring, they seemed to me to contain a horrid mockery, though to the native they no doubt appear the promptings of an affectionate and anxious solicitude. They are also supposed to contain a certain mystical meaning.

CREIGHTON AND SCALES, PRINTERS, O'CONNELL STREET, AUCKLAND.